THE

MAGIC

COMPASS

To.
Iain

Good Reading
and

Happy Holidays !

Doglas H Brown.
October 2, 2001

THE MAGIC COMPASS

Douglas Arthur Brown

Sydney, Cape Breton

Illustrations by Bruce J. Brown
Printed by City Printers, Sydney, Cape Breton

First published in Canada 1998 by Solus Publishing, Cape Breton, Nova Scotia

Second Edition 2001 Stork & Press

© Copyright Douglas Arthur Brown, 1998

Stork & Press
PO Box 40, Station A
Sydney, NS
B1P 6G9 Canada
902-567-6609 (telephone & facsimile)

Book and cover design by Pat O'Neil, Sydney
Cover artwork by Bruce J. Brown
Printed and bound in Cape Breton

Canadian Cataloguing in Publication Data

Brown, Douglas Arthur

    The magic compass

    ISBN 1-896792-05-7

1. Christmas stories, Canadian (English).*   1. Title.

PS8553.R68498M3 1998   jC813'.54   C98-950215-5
PZ7.B8133Ma 1998

FOR

Aaron, Arlen, Dylan, Eric, Jarret, Meghan,
Mitchell, Vanessa, Victoria & Zoe

ACKNOWLEDGEMENTS

The author and publisher would like to express their gratitude to
Jane Buss, Executive Director of the Writers' Federation of Nova Scotia, for her
continuing guidance and support.

The author wishes to extend special thanks to Lars Willum for his encouragement and support, and to the wizards in his life, his parents, Jenny and
Brent Brown.

THE FIRST DAY OF DECEMBER

In a corner of the Island Kingdom, Pendulum, the watchmaker, was fast asleep. His home and his workshop were in the White Palace, one of the many palaces in the Island Kingdom.

Pendulum had been working on a mechanical toy since September. The toy was a gift for his nephew, Clipper, who lived in the Nisse Palace on the other side of the Kingdom. There were only two or three springs to tighten up and a handful of latches and levers to be oiled before the toy was finished. Pendulum had been tinkering for months and was now fast asleep.

He had been asleep for three weeks, but for a Nisse, three weeks was just a nap.

The clocks in his workshop ticked away. Tick-tock. Tick-tock. The chimes sent the window blinds flapping, letting in the first sunbeams of December. The sun's rays bounced off the shiny surfaces of the dozens of clocks that filled the room.

Pendulum awoke with a start. He rubbed his sleepy eyes and put on his long pointed Nisse hat, which had fallen off during the nap. Crossing the room, he looked at the calendar.

"Tighten my gaskets," he said, "it's the first day of December. It's time to wind my clocks."

> *Tick-tock   Tick-tock*
> *I hear the voice of the clock*
> *Ticking all the hours away*
> *I must hurry or lose the day*
>
> *Tick-tock   Tick-tock*
> *I think all the springs are locked*
> *A dab of oil a little grease*
> *I must hurry or have no peace*
>
> *Tick-tock   Tick-tock*
> *December is here*
> *To bring us good cheer*
>
> *Tick-tock*

In another corner of the Island Kingdom, in the Nisse Palace, Balto and his wife, Tandara, sat filling sacks with rice.

"That's the last one," Balto said, wiping his brow. "We should have enough rice to last the month." He covered his round belly with his hand. His stomach growled.

"Is that your tummy roaring like a lion, Balto?" Tandara asked.

Pendulum in his workshop tinkering with his clocks

"It's all this rice. It makes me hungry."

"As soon as Clipper comes home, I'll set the table and we'll all sit down to a bowl of Rice Pudding—the first Rice Pudding of December," Tandara said proudly.

Nisses loved Rice Pudding.

No sooner had Tandara said this when Clipper came running into the room. He had been out all afternoon collecting berries to string into garlands for the Christmas tree and the arches of the Nisse Palace.

"I can smell Rice Pudding!" he shouted.

Soon they were all sitting around the table and Balto dished out a bowl of Rice Pudding for everyone. The clock on the wall chimed out the hour.

Tick-tock Tick-tock
I hear the voice of the clock
Ticking all the hours away
We must hurry or lose the day

Tick-tock Tick-tock
The rice is waiting
The pots are scrubbed
Boil the milk and grab a mug

Tick-tock Tick-tock
December is here
To bring us good cheer
Tick-tock

In a third corner of the Island Kingdom, the Royal Palace stood high on a hill. It was here the Prince lived with his wise wizard, Klo. The Prince had gathered all of his staff to hear reports on the preparations for Christmas. The Baker presented the Prince with a list of cakes, cookies and candies to be made in the Royal Kitchens. Pepper nuts, candy canes, sugar bells, and ribbon taffy were among the delights that the Baker recited from the long list. The Forester reported that the Christmas tree farms had produced a bumper crop of blue, red, green and white spruce, and fir trees and pine trees that could reach to the rafters.

The Prince listened to reports from everyone. He made an occasional change here and there, but generally he was satisfied. When everyone had given a report and left the room, the Prince looked up at his wizard, Klo, who sat at the opposite end of the long table.

"Do you have it?" the Prince asked anxiously.

"Yes, Your Majesty," Klo replied, taking from his pocket a mysterious looking object encased in glistening brass.

It was the Magic Compass. He placed it in the centre of the table. The Prince reached for the Compass, but Klo covered it with his hand.

"Your Majesty, are you sure you want to continue with this plan of yours?"

The Prince didn't hesitate. "Absolutely!"

Two months ago, the Prince had asked Klo to create the Magic Compass. A Compass that could make a palace disappear if the needle were pointed in its direction.

"Why do you want to make palaces disappear?" Klo had asked the Prince.

"Because I plan to build a new palace," he had replied.

Klo hadn't liked the idea then and he didn't like it now.

"Your Highness, may I remind you, there are twenty-three palaces and one castle in this Kingdom. Why do you want to build a new one?"

"Because it's a tradition, Klo. All the Kings before me built a new palace."

"But you're not a King, Prince," Klo corrected.

"Not yet, Klo. But on the day I become King I will have built the biggest and most beautiful palace in the Kingdom."

Klo shook his head in defeat. Although he was the Prince's guardian and advisor, he had no power to disobey his monarch. Reluctantly, he removed his hand and slid the Compass along the table toward the Prince.

And there was more activity throughout the Island Kingdom on this, the first day of December. Miranda, who was Klo's niece, was boarding a train. She had just finished her first year of university and was returning to the Royal Palace to spend the Christmas holidays with her uncle. Miranda had been away for almost a year. She missed her uncle and the Royal Palace. She even missed the Prince, though he had often teased her as a child.

Miranda smiled. No one knew she was coming home early for Christmas. It was going to be a surprise. She found a seat in the train by the window and looked out. The platform was full of people coming and going—passengers waiting to board, families saying goodbye, porters with their collars turned up against the December winds. The clock on the platform struck the hour and all the passengers checked their watches.

Tick-tock Tick-tock
I hear the voice of the clock
Ticking all the hours away
We must hurry or lose the day

Tick-tock Tick-tock
December is here
To bring us good cheer
Tick-tock

What will become of the Kingdom if the wizard allows the Prince to destroy some of the palaces? And what role will the Magic Compass play in the story that is about to unfold? Well, the story has just begun.

Until tomorrow, good night.

THE SECOND DAY OF DECEMBER

Winter had arrived on the Island Kingdom. The brooks were frozen, the small forest animals had grown thick furs, and the air was crisp. It was early morning and a fresh snow had fallen during the night. The sleigh carrying the Prince and Klo dashed through the forest toward the Blue Palace. The sleigh came to a halt in the courtyard.

The Blue Palace had not been inhabited for many years. The windows were shuttered and some of the bricks had fallen from the chimneys. The Prince and Klo climbed out of the sleigh.

"Are you certain this is what you wish, Your Highness?" Klo asked.

"Yes," answered the Prince. He removed the Compass from his pocket and opened it. The face was inscribed with twenty-four pictures. One for each of the twenty-three palaces and the one castle to be found in the Kingdom. Klo slowly wound the Compass until the needle pointed to the Blue Palace. With a sigh, he snapped the Compass shut.

The Blue Palace began to fade from sight. Soon it was gone, as though it had never been there. Klo shook his head and turned to the Prince.

"Your Highness, is it absolutely necessary that we proceed with your plan to make some of the palaces in the Kingdom disappear? These are palaces that have been in your family for generations."

"Most of these palaces are empty and old, Klo. I don't like old things. I want to build a new modern palace and have you make all the old palaces disappear," the Prince said.

Klo scratched his head. Had he heard the Prince correctly? Had the Prince said he wanted **all** the palaces to disappear?

"Yes, Klo, I want you to make all the palaces disappear. Not just some, but all of them," the Prince repeated.

Klo grew silent. The Prince had tricked him. If he had known the Prince had planned to make all the palaces disappear, and not just one or two, he would never have made the Magic Compass in the first place. And while he pondered this thought, another concern grew within him.

"What about the Nisses? Where will they live if you make all the palaces disappear?" Klo asked.

The Prince began to laugh.

The Prince using his Magic Compass for the first time

"I'm too old to believe in fairy tales. There are no Nisses."

"No Nisses?" Klo bellowed. "No Nisses? How dare you say that?"

The Prince stopped laughing. "I dare because I am the Prince. If I say there are no Nisses, then there are no Nisses," he said, folding his arms across his chest and turning his nose skyward.

Klo knew it was useless to argue with the Prince, but he had to protect the Nisses, even if the Prince didn't believe in them.

"But Your Highness, you have no experience building palaces. What if your creation fails? Where will you live if all the other palaces have disappeared?"

Once again the Prince began to smile, only this time it was more of a smirk than a real smile. "I've drawn up the plans for the new palace, Klo. You and your magic will build it. It will not fail."

There was nothing left to say. The Prince and Klo climbed into the sleigh, the silence between them was as chilly as the morning air.

From behind a bush, the Nisse, Tandara, watched the sleigh as it sped away. Tandara had travelled through the burrows that connected all the palaces in the Kingdom. She had come to the Blue Palace to gather some holly berries. When she saw the sleigh approach, she had hidden behind the bush. Nisses did not like to interfere with humans. They were shy and they liked to keep out of sight whenever humans were near. Tandara had heard everything the Prince and Klo had said. She had even seen the Blue Palace vanish.

"Balto won't be happy when he hears this news," she said, jumping into the burrows and heading homeward.

While Tandara was hurrying through the burrows to the Nisse Palace, Balto and Clipper were busy cleaning. The Nisse home had to be spick-and-span because Uncle Pendulum was coming to visit in a few days.

Balto opened the small windows and nodded to the sunny day. He took a deep breath of fresh air, then returned to his chores. He unlocked a cupboard and carefully removed a large book. It was the Nisse Hand Book. It held the answers to all the Nisses' questions. Very old and very fragile, it had been in the family for generations, passed down through the ages from mother to son, father to daughter. Balto carefully dusted the cover of the book then locked it away in the cupboard again.

As Balto turned the key in the lock, Tandara climbed up through the trap door in the floor that led to the burrows beneath the Nisse Palace. She was huffing and puffing.

"Tandara, why are you so out of breath?" Balto asked.

When she caught her breath, she told Balto and Clipper about the Magic Compass and the Prince's plan to make all the palaces in the Kingdom disappear. And then she told them about the Prince's plan to build a new palace.

"Why does the Prince need to build a new palace? There are already twenty-three in the Kingdom."

"There are only twenty-two now," Tandara corrected, and under her breath she added, "plus one castle."

"I think a new palace is exciting," Clipper said.

Balto and Tandara exchanged a worried look.

"Balto, I think you better explain to Clipper what this means," Tandara suggested.

"Explain what?" Clipper asked.

"Clipper, I know you think this is all very exciting, but it is very bad news for Nisses. The Prince plans to make all the palaces disappear, including the Nisse Palace—our home. It protects us from the...from the..."

"From what, Papa?"

Balto had no choice. He told Clipper about the Trolls of the Glen.

"The Trolls live in a castle on the far side of the Kingdom, in a place known as the Glen. Trolls don't like Nisses because we guard the Nisse Hand Book. And the Trolls want the Nisse Hand Book," Balto explained.

"Why?" Clipper asked.

"Because it's full of secrets and the Trolls always want to know secrets," Tandara said. "Luckily, the Trolls can't find the Nisse Hand Book because we keep it under lock and key here at the Nisse Palace. The Trolls can't find us or the Nisse Hand Book because the Nisse Palace is invisible."

"Invisible?" Clipper said.

"Yes," Balto said. "The Nisse Palace is invisible to the Trolls. As long as we are within the shadow of the Nisse Palace, the Trolls can't find us or the Nisse Hand Book."

"Every day the Trolls stare into their Vat of Boiling Milk, looking for the location of the Nisse Palace," Tandara added. "And every day they hope to catch one of us if we leave the safety of its shadow."

"But Mama," Clipper cried, "the Trolls must have seen you earlier today at the Blue Palace. The shadow of the Nisse Palace doesn't reach the Blue Palace."

"When I travel through the Kingdom, I use the burrows that run beneath all the palaces. The Trolls can't see anything that travels below the surface of the earth."

Clipper listened carefully to the story his parents were telling him. He found the Trolls even more exciting than the Prince's plan to build a new palace.

"Papa, if we go to live at the Prince's new palace, won't he protect us from the Trolls?"

Balto and Tandara exchanged another glance.

"I'm afraid not. The Prince doesn't believe in Nisses. He can't protect something he doesn't believe in."

"We'll just have to find a way to stop the Prince," Clipper said.

"I think there's a way," Tandara answered. "Pendulum is the finest watchmaker in the Kingdom. He'll help us."

"How can Pendulum help us?"

"The Magic Compass is made from springs, levers and latches. Pendulum can fix or unfix any mechanical device. He'll be able to stop the magic of the Compass," Balto explained. "When Pendulum comes to visit us, we'll tell him about the Magic Compass. He'll help us."

"Tell me more about the Trolls," Clipper said.

"We've already said enough," Tandara whispered. "If we let the Trolls walk around in our thoughts for too long, the Nisse Palace begins to lose some of its invisibility. Don't think about the Trolls anymore. Your curiosity will attract them."

And that was that. There was no more discussion about the Trolls of the Glen that evening. And as night descended over the Kingdom, the Nisse family ate their Rice Pudding and got ready for bed.

At the Royal Palace, the Prince had fallen asleep with the drawings for the new palace spread out upon his lap. Klo was snoring in his library chair, exhausted with worry over the safety of the Nisses. And in the distance, the whistle blew as the train, with Miranda on board, chugged toward the Royal Palace.

Miranda had fallen asleep from the gentle rocking of the train. She would be home by morning.

And somewhere in the Kingdom, two Trolls were also sleeping.

But talk of the Trolls can wait.

Until tomorrow, good night.

THE THIRD DAY OF DECEMBER

After her long train trip, Miranda arrived at the Royal Palace and stood in the centre of her uncle's library. She admired the rows of books that lined the walls from floor to ceiling and breathed in the familiar musty smell of the old manuscripts. It was the smell of her childhood. She loved this room. She turned to face the fireplace and stretched out her hands to warm them.

Silently a panel in the bookcase opened behind her and Klo entered the room. The panel slipped shut behind him. Klo was surprised to see his niece warming herself beside the fire.

"Miranda!" he cried, throwing open his arms.

Miranda swung around to face her uncle. "Uncle Klo, you scared me. Can't you enter a room by the door like everyone else?" she teased, rushing across the room to give her uncle a hug.

"Why are you home so early? I didn't expect you for another two weeks."

"Sit with me by the fire, Uncle Klo, and I'll tell you everything."

Klo looked suspiciously at his niece as they sat. "What do you mean, everything?"

"I've come home early to work on a school project. It's a project in architecture."

"Architecture?" Klo gasped. "I sent you away to school to become a wizard, not an architect."

"I wasn't a very good wizard. I couldn't cast spells and my potions never worked. Architecture is more interesting. I plan to become a first class architect, which is better than a second class wizard."

Klo made no comment.

"Now tell me everything that has happened since I left," Miranda said, filling the silence.

Klo started to tell Miranda about the Prince's plan to build a new palace.

"That's great news. A new palace in the Kingdom. That's even more exciting than my project."

"And just what project is that?"

"I want to do some renovations on the Nisse Palace. That's why I've come home early."

Klo shook his head. He told Miranda about the Magic Compass and the Prince's plan to make all the palaces in the Kingdom vanish. When Miranda heard of this plan, she jumped to her feet.

"He's nothing but an overgrown brat!"

"Miranda, show some respect. After all, he is the Prince."

"But Uncle Klo, I have plans to renovate all the palaces in the Kingdom."

Klo began to laugh. For as long as he could remember the Prince and Miranda had been competing with each other. He was happy that Miranda had come home early, even though her news about becoming an architect was not what he had expected.

"Maybe you can talk some sense into the Prince," Klo said.

"Well, I can't just let him destroy all the palaces in the kingdom," Miranda said. "I'll be out of a job. I planned to renovate one palace each year for the next twenty-four years. Can't you just reverse the magic of the Magic Compass?"

"The Magic Compass was made for the Prince. He's the only one who can reverse the magic. If anyone other than the Prince tinkers with it, they will turn to stone."

"Wait till I get my hands on him!"

"You've had a long journey, Miranda. Rest. Tomorrow the Prince will unveil his plans for the new palace. You can give him an earful then."

Klo kissed his niece and walked her to the door.

He returned to the fire and stared into the flames. There were suddenly so many things to worry about. He had looked forward to the day when he might retire and allow Miranda to become the new wizard in the Kingdom. But nothing was going as he had planned. The Prince wanted to destroy all the palaces and Miranda wanted to renovate them. Why couldn't they just leave things alone? And with these thoughts, Klo shut his eyes and fell into a troubled sleep.

Early that same evening Clipper was preparing for bed at the Nisse Palace. He had spent the day stringing holly berries to make garlands to hang from the arches and to drape on the Christmas tree. He had washed his hands over and over again. The holly berries had dyed the tips of his fingers a rosy red.

Balto and Tandara tucked Clipper into bed and blew out the candles. But Clipper couldn't sleep. He was thinking about the Trolls of the Glen. He had been thinking about them all day, forgetting what his parents had told him the night before. He had forgotten that he should not let the Trolls walk around in his thoughts for too long.

On the far side of the Kingdom, in the Glen, stood Troll Castle. And in the kitchen of the castle, two Trolls were snoring in their rocking chairs. Spike the dog lay at their feet. Suddenly, Fennika, the older of the two Trolls, awoke with a jump. She shook her brother.

"Wake up, Archibald, wake up!"

Archibald jumped from his chair. "Oh, Fennika," he said, "it's only you. I was having such a nice dream."

"Trolls don't have nice dreams, Archibald. They have nightmares. How many times do I have to tell you that?"

"Sorry, Fennika, I forgot."

"Never mind. There are more important things to discuss. Archibald, I heard the thoughts of a Nisse child."

Archibald began to look around the kitchen, excitedly. "A Nisse? Here? We haven't had guests in over a hundred years. Where is it?"

"It's not an *it*, it's a *him*, and he isn't here. I heard his thoughts in my big ears. Somewhere in the Kingdom, within the safety of the Nisse Palace, a little Nisse has been thinking about Trolls. Do you know what that means?"

Archibald clapped his hands. "It means we're going to have guests."

Fennika rolled her eyes. Archibald was a big disappointment, as far as Trolls went. He was kind and gentle, considerate and polite. He was everything Fennika hated in other creatures. She scampered across the big messy kitchen to the Vat of Boiling Milk which stood in the centre of the room.

"Archibald, fetch me the Troll powder!" she shouted.

Fennika had many different powders lining the shelves of the kitchen. There were sneezing powders, itching powders, flea powders and the one she needed now. Archibald reached up to the top shelf and fetched the powder Fennika wanted. It was a powder that would allow her to see the thoughts of other creatures. She sprinkled the powder into the Vat of Boiling Milk.

"Can you see the Nisse, Fennika, can you?" Archibald asked from over Fennika's shoulder.

"No, I can't see anything. The little creature must have fallen asleep. I can't look into dreams. But tomorrow, when he wakes up, maybe he'll think about us again. I'll see him in my Vat of Boiling Milk and then I'll know where the Nisse Palace is hidden. And do you know what that means, Archibald?"

"It means the Nisses are in big trouble."

"Exactly. When I know where the Nisse Palace is, I will know where the Nisse Hand Book is. And when I have the Nisse Hand Book, I will have all their secrets."

"What secrets are those, Fennika?"

"That's what a secret is. Something to discover." Fennika began to laugh.

Archibald rubbed one foot behind the other. "Fennika, since you're in a good mood—do you think this year, that...maybe...we could get a Christmas tree?"

Fennika jumped up and down.

"A Christmas tree? How many times have I told you? Trolls are allergic to Christmas trees!"

Spike looked up at her and growled.

"There, there, doggy, take it easy," she said.

Fennika didn't like dogs and they didn't much like her.

"Take that mutt for a walk, Archibald. I'm going to bed. I want to be well rested so I can think up ways to catch the Nisses." She stomped out of the kitchen and slammed the door behind her.

Archibald waited until he was sure she was gone before he went to a cupboard in the corner of the kitchen. He opened the door and took out a tiny Christmas tree, no more than a foot high. He placed the tiny tree on the centre of the table. It drooped slightly to the side of the pot.

> *In a forest In a glen*
> *In a field Or fox's den*
> *There grows a seed*
> *A little each day*
> *Bursting forth on the first of May*
>
> *Through rains of Spring*
> *And Summer's warmth*
> *Under Autumn's cloak*
> *and wind from North*
> *The little seed grows strong and tall*
> *Until that day it decks the hall*
>
> *Balls of glass*
> *Sparkle on green*
> *Presents wrapped with all our dreams*
> *Candy canes dangle*
> *And strings of berries*
> *Adorn your figure*
> *To make us merry*

The little Christmas tree continued to droop and Archibald sighed. Spike barked and pointed at his water bowl.

"Are you thirsty, Spike?" Archibald asked.

Spike shook his head and pointed his paw at the little tree.

"Of course, maybe the tree is thirsty." Archibald gave the little tree some water from Spike's bowl and immediately it straightened up.

"What a clever dog you are, Spike. Come on, let's go for that walk." Archibald put the leash around Spike and headed for the door.

"Oops. I almost forgot, I can't let Fennika find my Christmas tree," he said and returned the little tree to the cupboard.

"Until tomorrow," he whispered and took Spike outside.

What adventures were in store for Archibald tomorrow? And what about the Nisses? Would Fennika find them through the magic of her Troll powders and the Vat of Boiling Milk? And would the Prince continue to make the other palaces in the Kingdom vanish before Christmas?

Until tomorrow, good night.

Archibald and his Christmas Tree

THE FOURTH DAY OF DECEMBER

As promised, the Prince summoned Miranda and Klo to the unveiling of the model for his new palace.

"Are you ready?" the Prince asked, holding one corner of the satin cloth that covered it.

"Yes, yes," replied Klo impatiently.

Miranda nodded her head, and the Prince lifted the cloth from the model. She was amazed. She hadn't expected the model to be so elaborate.

"Forty rooms!" boasted the Prince. "Over here is the indoor swimming pool—complete with dolphins."

The Prince pointed to the recording studio on the second floor. In the east wing there was a video arcade. In the west wing, a pizza parlour. All the hallways had mini-golf putting greens along the sides. And instead of stairs, there were escalators.

"It looks more like a shopping mall than a palace," Klo grumbled.

"There are still some kinks to be worked out, but generally I think it's pretty good for a first effort," the Prince said, ignoring Klo's criticism.

"What are you going to call it?" Miranda asked.

"Well, since this is December I think I'll call it the Christmas Palace. So, what do you think of it, Miranda?"

"I'm not sure. Speaking as a future architect, I think it could be either a dream come true or a total nightmare. Either way, it is impressive."

Klo was not impressed. "Your Highness, I have served this family for many generations. I've served your father and his father before him. I have never had reason to question the judgement of my monarch until today. Your plan to destroy all the beautiful palaces in the Kingdom and to replace them with this flimsy tinsel fortress is ridiculous."

The Prince did not take kindly to criticism. Still, Klo was his trusted advisor and guardian. "I admit it has some rough spots, but you can tidy it up with your magic, Klo," the Prince said, grinning.

"You don't understand, Your Highness. I must disobey you. I will not build this palace."

The Prince was no longer grinning. He didn't know what to say so he ended up saying the wrong thing. "If you won't build my new palace, I will confine you to your rooms. You are now under house arrest."

"So be it," Klo said and prepared to leave the room.

"And don't go getting any ideas about casting a spell over me to make me change my mind," the Prince shouted. "Now that I have made you a prisoner of the Royal Palace, your magic has no power over me."

It was the truth. Klo had become a prisoner and had lost all his magical powers over the Prince.

Miranda watched silently as two guards escorted Klo out of the room. Then she exploded. "You're a bully, Your Highness! You always were and you always will be."

"Come on, Miranda, lighten up. Klo will come to his senses. In a couple of days he'll calm down and everything will get back to normal."

"Haven't you learned anything from Uncle Klo?" Miranda asked, impatiently. "He never changes his mind once he's made a decision. Your new palace will never be built."

"It will be built, Miranda. It will be built and finished by Christmas."

Miranda flashed an angry glance at the Prince. "What do you mean?"

"Klo told me you switched your studies at school. He said you want to become an architect. He also told me you've come home early to work on a project."

"So?"

"What could be more glamorous than building my Christmas Palace? When you go back to school, all the other students will be green with envy."

Miranda's heart began to pound. It was true. Building the Prince's Christmas Palace would certainly be more of a challenge than redecorating the Nisse Palace. The idea excited her. But then she remembered her uncle. She could never go against his wishes. And this she told the Prince.

The Prince regarded Miranda for a long moment before answering. "If you don't build my new palace, I'll put you under house arrest too, and you'll never become an architect. Do you understand?"

Miranda understood all too well. "Very well, Your Highness. I'll do your bidding," she said formally. "I'll build your new palace, but under one condition."

"And what might that be?" the Prince said with a smirk.

"You give me permission to say what's on my mind."

"Fire away."

And fire away she did.

"You're all those things the people in the Kingdom whisper about you—only worse. You're a tyrant. You haven't changed one bit since I saw you last," she said, pausing to catch her breath. "Do you remember all those times we played hopscotch when we were kids? I let you win so you wouldn't howl like a baby and wet your Royal Drawers when you lost."

The Prince was not happy. No one had ever spoken to him like that before. He looked at the model of the Christmas Palace. It no longer looked as grand or exciting as it had earlier in the day.

The Prince took the Magic Compass from his pocket. He set the arrow over the Orange Palace on the dial and snapped the Compass shut.

"My Christmas Palace will be the only one in the Kingdom," he shouted, as the Orange Palace, far across the Kingdom, vanished.

Meanwhile, at Troll Castle on the other side of the Kingdom, Fennika was stirring her Vat of Boiling Milk. She was hoping to get a glimpse of the Nisse child who had been thinking about Trolls the night before.

"Do you see him?" Archibald asked, still excited about the possibility of guests visiting the castle.

"No, he hasn't been thinking about us today. But soon. I'll just sit here and wait."

And Fennika waited. She waited all day, watching the bubbles in her Vat of Boiling Milk, looking for a sign of the Nisse who could lead her to the Nisse Palace.

While Fennika searched her Vat of Boiling Milk for a sign of Clipper, Pendulum, the watchmaker, was out in the courtyard of the White Palace where he lived. Normally, he would not venture from the safety of his workshop, but the events of the last couple of days had disturbed him.

Earlier that morning, Pendulum had travelled through the burrows that linked all the palaces in the Kingdom. When the Nisses travelled underground, the Trolls couldn't see them. He liked to visit the empty palaces which were filled with old broken clocks with many useful parts. Today he had gone to the Orange Palace to collect some screws and levers. But when he popped up from the burrows, the Orange Palace was nowhere to be found.

"First it was the Blue Palace," he said, "yesterday it was the Yellow Palace, and today the Orange Palace. If this continues, there will be no palaces left by Christmas. I bet this is the work of the Trolls of the Glen. It's a good thing I'm spending Christmas with the Nisses. We'll find a way of putting an end to the tricks of the Trolls."

Suddenly the clocks in Pendulum's workshop struck the hour.

"I've been outside too long. I hope the Trolls haven't picked up my scent." Pendulum hurried inside the White Palace to the safety of his workshop.

But Pendulum had, indeed, lingered too long in the courtyard—long enough for Fennika to see him in her Vat of Boiling Milk and to hear of his plan to visit the Nisse Palace. Fennika would pay a visit of her own. She would visit the White Palace tomorrow and meet Pendulum face to face.

Tandara, Balto and Clipper, stringing Christmas garlands

Back at the Nisse Palace, Clipper was still busy stringing the berries and popcorn into garlands.

"Is it tomorrow that Uncle Pendulum comes to visit?" Clipper asked for the tenth time that day.

"Yes, Clipper," Tandara answered patiently, "but there are still a dozen things to do. Let's start by hanging these garlands."

All you need is needle and thread
A bowl of popcorn
And berries I said
Start with the needle
And loop the thread
Oops turn it around
I meant the head

Through the popcorn
Easy you see
Then string the berries
One two three
Continue your chore
And before you know
Look at your feet
They've covered the floor

Garlands Garlands
Berries red and black
Garlands Garlands
Enough to fill ten sacks

It had been another chaotic day in the Kingdom. And tomorrow promises to be the same. How long will Klo be confined to his chambers? What plan does Fennika have in store for Pendulum? Can Miranda really finish the new palace by Christmas?

Until tomorrow, good night.

FIFTH DAY OF DECEMBER

Fennika had stayed up all night tending her Vat of Boiling Milk and blending her powders in the kitchen at Troll Castle. She was looking for just the right combination—of a little bit of this, a little bit of that.

Finally, as the first rays of morning sun crept into the dingy kitchen, Fennika let out a cry, "I've done it! I've done it! I've made a camouflage powder!"

"What's a camouflage powder?" Archibald asked, struggling to pronounce the strange word.

"It's a magic powder that lets me disguise myself as another creature."

"Why would you want to do that?"

"So I can fool the Nisses into thinking I'm something else—a bird, a fish, even a Nisse! "

"Oh," Archibald said, as though he understood, although he really didn't.

"With this camouflage powder," Fennika explained, "I'll be able to take on the shape of the Nisse named Balto. Then, disguised as Balto, I'll visit Pendulum at the White Palace."

She handed the canister to Archibald. "Now stand on that stool and sprinkle this over my head while I say the magic words."

Archibald climbed onto the stool and shook the canister. The white sparkling powder fell like snowflakes over Fennika as she recited the spell.

Balto, Balto is his name—make me look just the same.

Soon she was completely covered.

"You look like a snowman," Archibald said. "How will you get the Nisse Hand Book, looking like a snowman?"

"It takes a few minutes for the powder to work," Fennika growled.

Her nose began to tickle from the powder that had landed in her nostrils. With a sudden shudder she exploded in a sneeze that sent Spike scrambling under the kitchen table.

When the dust settled, Archibald opened his eyes and looked at his sister in amazement.

"It worked!" Fennika cried. "I did it."

Archibald rubbed his eyes. The voice sounded like Fennika but she no longer looked like his sister. The powder had changed her. She was short and round with a hat and a little white beard.

"What do you think?" Fennika asked, spinning around so that Archibald could get a good look.

The Troll, Fennika, and her Vat of Boiling Milk

"I don't know what to think," Archibald answered. "I don't even know what you are."

"I'm a Nisse," Fennika answered. "Well, not a real Nisse, but the magic powder makes me look just like one."

"Oh, Fennika, you should wear that disguise all the time," Archibald said gleefully.

"Don't be ridiculous. Nisses are ugly. Pooh! Now pass me my powder pouch and get out of the way. I have to hurry to the White Palace. This disguise won't last forever."

Archibald passed Fennika the pouch which contained several canisters of Troll powders. He waved goodbye as she left the castle.

"I wish there was something I could do to help the little Nisses, Spike," Archibald said. "Fennika is up to no good. She's probably going to capture that poor Nisse who lives at the White Palace, then take him here and throw him in the dungeon."

Then he smiled. "Or maybe Fennika will have a change of heart and let me have the Nisse as a friend. It gets so lonely around here sometimes without a friend."

Spike looked at Archibald with his big wet eyes and began to whimper.

"Sorry, Spike. Of course, you're my friend. You're my best friend. But it would also be nice to make friends with a Nisse. Then I would have two friends. We could have twice as much fun."

One friend sure is better than none
Two friends just double the fun
Candy tastes better when you're two
So tuck a piece in your shoe
My friend always makes me smile
When I'm sad every once in awhile

Two friends sure are better than none
Three friends just triple the fun
Making mudpies is better when you're three
Especially if you drop them from up in a tree
My friends always make me smile
When I'm sad every once in awhile

While Archibald was thinking about making new friends, Miranda was dining with her uncle at the Royal Palace.

"Miranda, you aren't eating your lunch."

"I'm not hungry."

"You have to eat to keep up your strength if you're going to build the Christmas Palace," he said.

"But I don't want to build the palace," Miranda answered, softly, toying with the peas on her plate.

Klo knew Miranda wanted more than anything else to build the palace. "Now listen to me, Miranda. As long as I am under house arrest, I can't use my magic powers. I may need your assistance. You must build this Christmas Palace. You won't be much help to me if you're also under house arrest. Agreed?"

Miranda was silent for a moment, finally she said, "Alright, Uncle Klo, I'll do it for you. But I don't understand why you let the Prince bully you the way he does."

Klo began to chuckle. "This isn't the first time the Prince has clipped my wings."

Miranda looked up from her plate. "You mean he's treated you like this before?"

"Many times. It's important for me to rebel once in a while to show the Prince that other people have opinions different from his own. Usually these lock-ups are short and don't interfere too much with my work. But this time I'm worried. I think the Trolls of the Glen are up to no good and I'm powerless to stop them."

"The Trolls of the Glen?"

"Yes, I think they plan to steal the Nisse Hand Book from the Nisse Palace. The Nisses are in great danger. And all because of the Magic Compass."

Now Miranda was really confused. "The Magic Compass? What does that have to do with Nisses?"

"If I hadn't made the Magic Compass, the Nisses would be safe."

Miranda began to laugh. "Oh, Uncle Klo. You haven't told me stories about the Nisses since I was a child. Those bedtime stories always helped me to fall asleep. But I'm an adult now."

Klo sighed. He remembered that neither Miranda nor the Prince believed in Nisses or Trolls. He would have to find a way to help his Nisse friends on his own.

"I'm going to go and tell the Prince that I will build his Christmas Palace," Miranda said, getting up from the table.

She kissed her uncle on the cheek and turned toward the door. "Brrr, it's chilly in here," she said. As she passed the fireplace, she snapped her fingers and the logs burst into a roaring fire. "That's better."

"And you try to tell me you're a second class wizard," Klo grumbled. "You have more magic in your fingertips than I had in my whole body at your age. It'll be interesting to see if you're as good an architect as you are a magician, Miranda."

She left the room, wondering the same thing.

Pendulum had finished packing for his trip to the Nisse Palace. It was always a pleasure to spend the holidays with Balto, Tandara and Clipper. Pendulum loved seeing the expression on Clipper's face with each new mechanical toy his uncle made for him.

But Pendulum was also eager to have a word with his brother, Balto, about the mysterious disappearance of the palaces. He was sure it had something to do with the Trolls of the Glen.

He sat at his table in the workshop and ate some cheese. It was important to have something in his tummy before the long journey. As he put the first mouthful to his lips, he heard a knock on the door and went to the window and peeked out.

"Tighten my gaskets, it's Balto!" Pendulum said to himself, puzzled. "But why is he here? I'm supposed to visit *him*."

He swung open the door to greet his brother. "Come in, Balto, come in."

Balto (that is, Fennika, disguised as Balto) looked around at the clocks ticking in the workshop. "What pretty clocks," she said in her nasal voice.

"Balto, you sound as though you have a cold. Come and have a piece of cheese. It always helps to clear up colds."

Fennika sat at the table and sniffed at the block of cheese. In one gulp, she downed the entire plate.

"You must have been very hungry after your trip," Pendulum said.

"Yes, yes. Hungry," Fennika answered.

"Balto, did you come here because of all the strange things happening the last couple of days."

"Yes, yes, strange things, but first, more food."

Pendulum passed her another slice of cheese. "My, what a fine tail you have, Balto," he said, admiring the long furry tail that peeked out from Balto's trousers. "Wait a minute, Nisses don't have tails!"

And before Pendulum could say anything more, Fennika opened her pouch and sprinkled him with sleeping powder. He fell fast asleep.

"Sweet dreams, Pendulum," she said, stuffing him into a sack and hoisting it onto her shoulders.

"That was close. The camouflage powder must be starting to wear off."

She glanced in a mirror and saw her old familiar self coming back. "Not a minute too soon."

She took one long look at the room and spied Pendulum's shiny oiling can sitting on the bench. Trolls loved to collect shiny things.

"What's this?" she wondered, testing the oil with her tongue. It tasted good, and she stuffed the oiling can in the sack with Pendulum and left the White Palace.

What plans did Fennika have for Pendulum? And what would the Nisses of the Nisse Palace do when Pendulum failed to show up for Christmas? And if Miranda didn't believe in Nisses, how could she help Klo?

Until tomorrow, good night.

THE SIXTH DAY OF DECEMBER

Miranda was spending the day at her drafting table, studying the sketches the Prince had given her for the Christmas Palace. She was eager to get started on the blueprints. Page after page of sketches were spread out in front of her and her eyes were getting tired. The drawings were all starting to look alike.

She was beginning to wonder if the task of building the Christmas Palace might be too big for her. There were still so many things she had to learn about architecture. The Prince had drawn sketches of the palace from every angle. Miranda admired his skill. The sketches for the Christmas Palace were good.

She rubbed her eyes, then rested her head on the table to take a little nap. Half an hour later the Prince came along to check on her progress. He found Miranda fast asleep. He tiptoed up behind her and tickled her in the ribs. Miranda jumped.

"Scared you, didn't I?" the Prince said grinning. "How's the work coming?"

Miranda scowled. "I'm slowly getting to the blueprints."

"Well, don't be too slow. Remember, the palace has to be finished by Christmas. You can always take a few shortcuts along the way."

"There are no shortcuts. If you had gone to university, you'd know that," Miranda snapped. She was tired and irritable.

"I don't have to go to university. I'm the Prince. Who could teach me how to become a Prince?"

"Have you ever thought of becoming something other than a Prince?" Miranda asked.

"I like who I am. I'm a good Prince."

"A good Prince wouldn't lock up his wizard just because he chose to disagree. And a good Prince wouldn't make all the palaces vanish just because he's afraid of the competition."

"Afraid of what competition?" the Prince asked, growing tired of their argument. He had hoped to find Miranda in a good mood, perhaps even convince her to take a walk. Instead she was grumpy.

"You're afraid that the people of the Kingdom might not like your palace," Miranda said.

"I don't care what anybody thinks, I'm the ..."

"I know, I know—you're the Prince."

Miranda knew it was useless to argue with him. She sighed and turned her attention back to the sketches.

Miranda studying the Prince's sketches

❄

Tandara and Balto were peeking out the window of the Nisse Palace. There was still no sign of Pendulum.

"Come on Tandara, it's time to eat, we can't wait any longer," Balto said. "The Rice Pudding is getting cold."

Balto and Tandara joined Clipper at the dinner table to eat their Rice Pudding, occasionally glancing at the empty place that had been set for Pendulum.

"Why isn't Pendulum here yet?" Clipper asked.

"Pendulum gets confused sometimes, dear. He probably took a wrong turn along the way. Remember the last time he visited us? He arrived wearing his pyjamas. He'd been so excited, he forgot to change his clothes before he left."

"Don't worry. I'm sure he'll be here tomorrow." Balto said, and they all took a spoonful of Rice Pudding in silence.

Clipper wasn't convinced. It was true that Pendulum was often confused, but he was never late for a Christmas visit. Pendulum was a watchmaker. He was surrounded by clocks. Like all good watchmakers, Pendulum was always punctual.

The Nisses finished their meal and washed the dishes. Several garlands still waited to be hung about the room. The smell of fresh boughs and berries filled the air.

"Remember, we must leave one garland for Pendulum to hang. It's a tradition," Tandara said, admiring the decorations. "Now off to bed, Clipper. I'm sure Pendulum will be here when you wake up in the morning."

❄

Tandara was wrong. Fennika had carried Pendulum to Troll Castle. Archibald and Spike stood beside her in the dungeon as she dumped him out of the sack onto the hard, cold floor.

"A real Nisse! We're going to be such good friends," Archibald shouted, clapping his hands.

"Trolls can't be friends with Nisses. Trolls don't like Nisses. How many times have I told you that?" Fennika snapped.

"I've never met a Nisse before. Maybe we'll like each other," Archibald said.

Fennika shook her furry paw at Archibald.

Nisses are sweet and round and soft
They smile all day and clean the loft
Their homes are filled with light and joy
Good little girls and proper little boys

But Trolls are fat and ugly too
Hold your breath while I take off my shoe
We like spiders and a dirty room
Whoever saw us with a broom

Nisses are polite and never lie
They never complain they're pleasant as pie
*They greet each other with a **how-do-you-do***
They even take baths yes that too

But Trolls are rotten to the core
Close that window and shut that door
Fresh air makes us sniff and sneeze
Whoever heard a Troll say please

"What's his name?" Archibald asked, carefully stepping closer to get a better look at their guest.

"His name is Pendulum."

"Pendulum, what a great name," Archibald said, noticing the shiny oiling can that lay beside Pendulum on the floor.

"What's this?" Archibald asked, picking up the oiling can.

"It's some kind of Nisse juice," Fennika answered, snatching the oiling can from Archibald's paws. She squirted a few drops into her mouth. "You wouldn't like it." She stuffed the oiling can into her pocket.

"Fennika, can I stay here with the Nisse and guard him?" Archibald asked.

"You? Do you think I'm out of my mind. You couldn't guard your own shadow. You're even afraid to walk past the family portraits in the Troll Gallery. You can't do anything like a Troll."

It was true. Archibald wasn't very good at doing any of the normal things Trolls were noted for. He didn't like to growl, or knit his eyebrows in a grimace. He didn't like to take temper tantrums and turn blue. And, as Fennika said, he was afraid to pass by the portraits that hung on the walls of the castle. They all looked mean and grumpy.

"Let's go upstairs," Fennika said. "Pendulum won't wake up from my sleeping powder until tomorrow. Spike, stay here and guard the Nisse."

Archibald and Fennika left the cell, locking the door behind them. Their shuffling footsteps disappeared down the corridor. Pendulum stopped snoring and opened his eyes. He wasn't really asleep, he was just pretending. Fennika hadn't given him enough sleeping powder.

"What a predicament I've gotten myself into," he muttered, sitting up and brushing the straw from his clothes. "Imagine me, Pendulum, being tricked by a Troll."

Spike gave a little bark and Pendulum leapt onto the bed in the corner of the cell, his knees trembling.

"Nice doggy, easy boy, nice doggy. Don't you go getting any ideas about eating me. Nisses taste terrible."

But Spike began to wag his tail, jumped onto the bed, and licked Pendulum's face.

"You're a friendly little fellow," Pendulum said, scratching Spike behind the ear. "You must belong to that other Troll. I think we can be good friends, you and I."

Pendulum looked around the cell for a way out. But there was no window. "I have to get out of this dungeon and warn the Nisses at the Nisse Palace," he thought.

He hopped off the bed and went to the door of the cell. He shook the bars but they wouldn't budge. He was locked in tight.

"I suppose there's nothing for me to do but wait. I'm sure the Trolls have some plan up their sleeve."

He stretched his arms and yawned. "I guess I still have a little bit of that sleeping powder in my nose. I'll just catch up on my sleep until I know what they want from me. I'll think clearer in the morning."

Pendulum yawned again and stretched out on the bed with Spike curled up at his feet.

Everyone in the Kingdom was preparing for another night's sleep, except Klo. He sat in front of the fireplace staring into the flames.

"So, the Trolls have captured Pendulum and taken him to Troll Castle, have they?" he said to himself.

Although Klo was under house arrest, he was still able to gaze into the flames of his fireplace and see everything that was happening in the Kingdom. Just as Fennika could look into her Vat of Boiling Milk and search for Nisses, Klo was able to look into his fireplace and search for Trolls. But Klo could not hear what the Trolls said. He could only guess from the glimpses he saw.

"Well, it would appear that Pendulum is safe for the moment. The Trolls haven't hurt him. He's just a little groggy from the sleeping powder. But that will pass," Klo said, yawning. "I think the wind has carried some of that sleeping powder throughout the Kingdom. I better go to bed too."

Will Miranda be able to finish the blueprints in time to build the new palace by Christmas? And will Pendulum be able to find a way to get out of the Trolls' dungeon?

Until tomorrow, good night.

THE SEVENTH DAY OF DECEMBER

Pendulum was two days late for his Christmas visit to the Nisse Palace. Balto made a decision—he would go to the White Palace himself to fetch his brother.

"Papa," Clipper asked, "is it possible that the Prince has made the White Palace vanish with his Magic Compass?"

"That's a thought that never crossed my mind," Balto said. "All the more reason to hurry."

"Papa," Clipper continued, "what if the Nisse Palace vanishes while you're away? Would we vanish too?"

Balto scratched his jaw. This was also a possibility. "We'll all go to the White Palace," he said. "Hurry and get ready."

They each packed a small cloth sack and tied it to the end of a pole. They hoisted the poles over their shoulders. The sacks were filled with lots of Rice Pudding to keep them fed on their trip to the White Palace.

Balto opened the trap door in the floor of the Nisse Palace. "Watch your heads," he cautioned, as they all climbed down the ladder leading to the burrows. When everyone was safely below, Balto shut the trap door.

"Can I light the torch?" Clipper asked.

"We don't need torches in the burrows," Balto said. "There's always light."

And as Clipper stepped from the ladder into the burrows, he could see it was true. "But how can there be light when there is no sun or torches?" Clipper asked.

"The walls of the burrows are studded with light stones," Tandara explained.

Clipper examined the walls. Sure enough, they were covered with small white stones that shone like hundreds of tiny bright lights. The burrows ran beneath all the palaces in the Kingdom. They had been built many generations ago.

"Who built these tunnels?" Clipper asked.

"No one knows," Tandara answered. "Nisses have always used them to travel from one palace to another. They protect us from the roving eyes of the Trolls of the Glen. When the Trolls look into their Vat of Boiling Milk, they can't see anything that moves in the burrows."

At noon, the Nisses had reached a crossroads. They decided to stop and have their lunch. Tandara served Rice Pudding. When they finished eating, they continued on their way. The crossroads was marked with two signs, and the travelling Nisses took the road to the White Palace.

"If we keep a good pace, we should be there by supper," Balto said.

The thought of dinner made his stomach growl, even though he had just finished lunch.

"It sounds like thunder," Clipper remarked, laughing.

"It's just my stomach," Balto said, blushing.

Tandara and Clipper grinned and followed Balto through the burrows.

At the same time the Nisses reached the crossroads, Archibald unlocked the door to the cell deep in the dungeons of Troll Castle.

"I've brought you some nice cold soup," he said, offering the bowl to Pendulum.

Pendulum took a big gulp of the soup. It was cold and not very tasty. "You Trolls could learn a thing or two about making soup," he said, thinking about the hot Rice Pudding waiting for him at the Nisse Palace.

"If you don't like the soup, I can make you something else," Archibald offered.

"Why are you being so nice to me?"

"Because you are our guest and we never have guests. I want to be your friend," Archibald said.

"Friend? A Troll! Why would a Troll want to be friends with a Nisse?"

"Because I would like to have more friends. Spike and I are good friends. Do you want to be my friend? We're not all bad. Trolls have a good side too."

Archibald
Trolls are strong and very brave
We're not sad on rainy days
We like to cook and make a stew
Have you ever tasted boiled glue
Trolls have a good side too

Pendulum
But Trolls are fat and ugly—pew
I'll hold my breath if you take off your shoe
You like spiders and a dirty room
Whoever saw a Troll with a broom

Archibald
Trolls have eyes that see at night
They even sparkle at day's first light
We brush our fur from foot to head
Sometimes we even make our bed
Trolls have a good side too

Pendulum
But Trolls are rotten to the core
Closing windows and slamming doors
Fresh air makes them sniff and sneeze
Whoever heard a Troll say please

Archibald
Some Trolls make lifelong friendships
Just ask Spike about our kinship
Trolls have a good side too

While Archibald and Spike were busy making friends with Pendulum, Fennika was upstairs in the kitchen stirring her Vat of Boiling Milk. Although she could see no sign of Balto, Tandara or Clipper, she had a plan.

"Sooner or later the Nisses will start looking for Pendulum when he doesn't arrive for his Christmas visit. When they do, I'll be ready for them. I'll make them take me back to the Nisse Palace, where I'll find the Nisse Hand Book."

Fennika gave the Vat of Boiling Milk another stir and sat back in her rocking chair to review her plan.

As the sun set that evening, the Nisse family emerged from the burrows beneath the White Palace. They went directly to Pendulum's workshop.

"Look Mama," Clipper said, "the table is scattered with crumbs."

"There's something mysterious about all of this," Tandara said.

Balto removed a magnifying glass from his sack and walked around Pendulum's workbench. Suddenly he stopped and gasped.

"What is it, Papa? What have you found?" Clipper asked.

"This is a sorry state of affairs. A sorry state of affairs, indeed."

"What is it?" Tandara asked.

Balto held up a long stiff bristle between his fingers. It looked like a piece of straw from a wicker broom. But Balto knew it was from the fur of a Troll!

"What does it mean, Papa?"

"The Trolls are always shedding, leaving a trail of fur behind them. They've been here and probably captured Pendulum."

"What should we do?" Clipper asked.

"We have to go back to the Nisse Palace and consult the Nisse Hand Book. We must find the route that will lead us to Troll Castle so we can rescue Pendulum," Tandara answered calmly.

"But we already know where the Trolls live. You told us yourself—they live in the Glen," Clipper said.

"Yes, but we don't know how to get there. Just as the Trolls can't find the Nisse Palace, we don't know where the Glen is. We have to find the route. When we've found it, we'll go to the Glen and rescue Pendulum."

"If Pendulum remains a prisoner, we'll never be able to get the Magic Compass and stop it from making the palaces vanish. Come on, we can't waste any more time," Tandara said.

The Nisses gathered their things and left Pendulum's workshop. They would return to the safety of the Nisse Palace through the burrows.

And in all the excitement, Clipper had not seen the mechanical toy standing in the corner of the workshop—the one Pendulum had made for him for Christmas. But Balto had seen it, and he carefully hid it in his sack to take back to the Nisse Palace.

The journey home to the Nisse Palace would take most of the night. Luckily, Balto had packed extra Rice Pudding. They would not be hungry.

Klo followed the actions of the Nisses in the flames of his fireplace. He knew they were headed back to the Nisse Palace. Once home, they would consult the Nisse Hand Book to find the path to Troll Castle. Klo looked at the calendar on his wall. It was already the seventh of December. He hoped the Nisses would be able to rescue Pendulum soon.

"Safe home, my little friends," Klo whispered into the flames as he prepared to retire for the night. "Until tomorrow," he said, snuffing the candle.

Will the Nisses be able to find the path to Troll Castle and rescue Pendulum? Will Fennika catch them before they do?

Until tomorrow, good night.

THE EIGHTH DAY OF DECEMBER

Clipper was catching up on his sleep after the long journey, but Balto and Tandara had not slept.

"There must be something in the Nisse Hand Book that can lead us to the Trolls of the Glen," Tandara said.

"But Tandara, we've been reading for hours and we still haven't found out where the Glen is located," Balto answered.

"I suppose we should just start from page one and read the entire book."

"But that will take days, the Nisse Hand Book is very thick," Balto said thoughtfully. "I don't know what else to do. If we don't find the answer soon, there's no telling what will happen to Pendulum."

Balto pondered the situation for a few minutes, then he said, "Clipper will be awake soon. I better make some lunch. We should take a break anyway, we've been reading all morning. After lunch, we'll be fresh again."

"I suppose you're right," Tandara replied as she was about to close the book. But at that moment her eye caught sight of something. "I found it!" she cried. " I found the passage that will lead us to Troll Castle."

Balto stood over her shoulder as she read.

> *If a Nisse should ever become a prisoner of the Trolls of the Glen, call upon the White Mare, for the White Mare can gallop across the sky from one end of the Kingdom to the other. She can see everything that lies below, including the Glen where the Trolls live.*

"Of course. I forgot all about the White Mare. She can take us to the Trolls of the Glen," Tandara shouted. "Tomorrow we'll call her and ask her to carry us there."

"How will we summon her?" Balto asked. Tandara consulted the book once again.

> *The White Mare can be summoned with two toots from a Nisse whistle.*

All Nisses carried a Nisse Whistle.

"Tomorrow morning I'll blow the whistle and she'll appear."

Tandara and Balto consulting the Nisse Hand Book

❄

While Balto and Tandara made their plans to find Pendulum, Miranda and the Prince were walking together down the long halls of the Royal Palace.

"Just a little further, Miranda, and we'll be there," the Prince said.

"This surprise better be worth it," Miranda said. "I'm missing valuable time at my drafting table."

"All work and no play isn't healthy, Miranda," the Prince said, "and you've been working hard, so you deserve a surprise."

"Well, I have to admit I do like surprises," Miranda confessed, as a smile formed at the corner of her mouth.

"I'm happy with the progress you've made on the Christmas Palace," the Prince said.

Miranda took advantage of the Prince's good humour. "Your Highness, since I'm doing your bidding, couldn't you release my uncle? I can't bear to see him locked up in that room day after day."

"I won't release him until he apologizes."

"It's you who should apologize. My uncle has served you loyally for a long time. He's been like a father to both of us, ever since your parents and mine passed away."

"I'm sorry, Miranda. I know this upsets you, but I must have discipline in my Kingdom. Besides, I think Klo expects it of me sometimes."

"You have absolutely no compassion. When our parents died, Klo raised us as if we were his own children. Is this how you repay his kindness?"

"Miranda, let's not fight again. Why can't we ever have a discussion without arguing?"

They had come to the tall doors at the end of the corridor. "Now close your eyes, we're here," the Prince said, "and give me your hand."

Miranda closed her eyes and held out her hand to the Prince. He opened the tall oak doors and they entered the room.

"You can look now, Miranda."

The room was ablaze with sparkling lights. Miranda couldn't believe her eyes. Dozens of Christmas trees filled the room, each decorated with hundreds of tiny candles. Miranda walked between the rows of pine and fir. She brushed against the silky boughs of the blue spruce and admired the two tall red spruces that reached to the ceiling, forty feet above her head. She bent and collected some of the cones that littered the floor. She happily breathed in the scent of the fresh sap.

"They're beautiful. I've never seen so many Christmas trees in my life. Where did they come from?"

"I had my Foresters collect trees from all over the Kingdom," the Prince replied. "I want you to pick the most beautiful tree of all. We'll use it as the first official Christmas tree in the new palace when I move in on Christmas Day."

Miranda stood back and let her eyes take in the forest before her. "They're all beautiful. It's difficult to choose one over the others."

She looked from tree to tree, settling finally on a fine red spruce hung with tiny silver snowflakes.

In a forest In a glen
In a field Or fox's den
There grows a seed
A little each day
Bursting forth on the first of May

Through rains of Spring
And Summer's warmth
Under Autumn's cloak
And wind from North
The little seed
Grows strong and tall
Until that day
It decks the hall

Balls of Glass
Sparkle on green
Presents wrapped with all our dreams
Candy canes dangle
And strings of berries
Adorn your figure
To make us merry

Later that afternoon, Clipper and Balto were gazing out over the Kingdom from the tower of the Nisse Palace.

"Clipper, let's find out which palace has vanished today," Balto said, putting the spyglass to his eye. Clipper looked at the list in his hands.

"Is it the Red Palace?" he asked.

Balto turned the telescope in the direction of the Red Palace. Its sparkling shape filled the telescope. "No. The Red Palace is still there."

Clipper continued down his list. "Is it the Green Palace?"

Balto searched the horizon for the Green Palace. The crescent shape of the high, thin palace came into view. "No, the Green Palace is still there."

"What about the Amber Palace?"

Once again Balto scanned the horizon. "Let's see, the Amber Palace would be over there." He pointed the telescope in the direction of the sun and the reflection of the Amber Palace almost blinded him. "No, the Amber Palace is still shining," he said, blinking.

"Then maybe it's the Turquoise Palace?" Clipper said, as he came to the bottom of his page.

"The Turquoise Palace? The Turquoise Palace is beside the Black Palace. Yes, there's the Black Palace—but no Turquoise Palace."

"Are you sure?" Clipper asked.

Balto looked again but he couldn't locate the Turquoise Palace. "It's gone."

Clipper put a mark through *The Turquoise Palace* on his list. He counted all the marks on his list. "First the Blue Palace, then the Yellow Palace, then the Orange Palace, the Crimson Palace, the Lilac Palace, the Pink Palace, and today the Turquoise Palace. Seven palaces have vanished."

Balto tucked the telescope into his belt.

"Papa, are you excited about visiting Troll Castle tomorrow?" Clipper asked.

"I'm excited about riding the White Mare, but I'm not excited about the Trolls," Balto said.

"Don't worry about those nasty Trolls," Clipper said, "I'll protect you."

Balto chuckled and gave his son a hug.

They heard Tandara calling them to dinner. They climbed on the railing and slid down the spiral stairway. Round and round they slid, down and down until they landed right in the middle of the Nisse kitchen.

"Wash your hands," Tandara said as she spooned out a double serving of Rice Pudding into each bowl.

At that moment, in the Royal Palace, Klo sat back in his comfortable chair in front of the fireplace. "Tomorrow the Nisses set out for Troll Castle," he mused. "I better put a couple of extra logs on the fire. I'll have to keep an eye on them all day."

He threw three logs onto the fire and glanced at his watch. "Miranda's late for dinner again," he said. "I hope she hasn't had another argument with the Prince."

But Miranda had spent the rest of the afternoon in the Christmas tree room with the Prince. They laughed and talked about everything that had happened to them over the past year.

And in the dungeon of Troll Castle, Archibald and Pendulum had become good friends and were playing a game of checkers.

Upstairs, Fennika was snoring away in her rocking chair as she dreamed about the Nisse Hand Book.

For one reason or another, everyone in the Kingdom was happy this night.

Until tomorrow, good night.

THE NINTH DAY OF DECEMBER

The Nisses were gathered in the courtyard. Tandara removed the whistle from around her neck. It was a special whistle, which only the creatures of the Kingdom could hear.

"Two short toots is the signal for the White Mare," Tandara said. So she gave the whistle two short toots.

"I can't hear anything," Clipper said, straining his ear to hear the approaching gallop of a horse.

"Be patient, it won't be long before she arrives."

> *The White Mare is the Nisse's friend*
> *Galloping high over hill and glen*
> *She tosses her mane to and fro*
> *Soars in the sky and swoops down low*
> *Her neck is long and slender and strong*
> *She trots with grace on winter's pond*
> *Her snowy coat glistens in morning's light*
> *A white bouquet in the moon's pale night*

And suddenly the White Mare appeared from the forest and cantered gracefully toward them.

"She's beautiful," Clipper exclaimed.

The White Mare was the most enchanting animal in the Kingdom. Her mane was braided with silver bells and her tail glistened like spun silk.

"Look!" Clipper shouted, "There, at the edge of the forest. Another one."

They all looked beyond the White Mare. At the edge of the pines, a young horse waited. It was the White Mare's colt. The White Mare signalled and the young colt came galloping toward her. Clipper took an apple from his pocket and fed it to the colt.

Balto passed each of them a pair of goggles. "It may get windy," he said.

"Clipper, you can climb onto the colt's back," Tandara said.

"The wind is at our backs and it's time to fly," Balto said.

Clipper mounted the colt and Tandara and Balto mounted the White Mare. The White Mare and her colt threw back their heads and whinnied. They were off at a gallop, and within seconds they had taken to the air.

These were no ordinary horses. The White Mare and her colt could gallop

Clipper on the back of the White Mare's colt

through the skies.

"Hurry-up, hurry-up," Clipper cried, as he held onto the colt's mane.

The White Mare and her colt banked to the left, jumping over a wispy cloud as they carried their passengers toward the Glen where the Trolls lived.

At Troll Castle, Fennika was gazing into her Vat of Boiling Milk. The Nisses had left the protection of the Nisse Palace and were no longer invisible. Fennika watched as they approached the Glen on the backs of the horses.

"This is what I've been waiting for!" she cried. "I have to prepare a special welcome for the Nisses when they arrive. Yes, a special welcome indeed."

Spike, who was watching Fennika from the corner of the kitchen, covered his eyes with his paws.

The White Mare and the colt continued to gallop through the skies. As the Nisses looked below, they noticed that the trees were dark and bare in this part of the Kingdom. The countryside was littered with big rocks and black bushes. The sun had disappeared behind a cloud.

"We must be getting close to the Glen," Balto shouted above the wind.

Suddenly both the White Mare and the colt rose on their hind legs and sniffed the air.

Tandara patted the White Mare's neck. "There, there, I know you smell danger. It's the scent of the Trolls. But we must keep going, White Mare. We have to rescue Pendulum."

The White Mare, calmed by Tandara's caress, continued her flight across the sky. But the colt had been frightened by the smell of danger and he rose farther back on his hind legs. Clipper slipped off his back. "Mama, I'm falling!" Clipper shouted as he tumbled through the air. But Tandara didn't hear him.

The colt followed the White Mare across the sky, not noticing that Clipper had fallen.

Clipper landed in a mud puddle in the middle of the forest. He stood up and looked around. All the trees in this part of the Kingdom were nothing but gnarled twisted branches. There wasn't a Christmas tree in sight.

"It certainly isn't very pretty around here," Clipper whispered to himself. "And I lost my mittens," he added, rubbing his fingers against the cold.

He looked around again, trying to figure out where he was. "I must be close to Troll Castle. I'll have to be very quiet," he whispered. "I can't let the Trolls know I'm here."

He tiptoed through the forest, but Fennika, who had been watching it all in her Vat of Boiling Milk, was expecting him. She had placed nets all through the forest. One net was hidden under a pile of leaves and Clipper stepped into it. It sprung up, trapping him inside.

"Help, help!" Clipper shouted. "Mama, Papa, I'm trapped!"

But Tandara and Balto were too high up in the sky to hear him.

Fennika stepped out from behind a tree. "Now I have you, my darling Nisse," she snarled. "Lucky for me you fell from that pony. You're a prisoner of the Trolls of the Glen. And I'm sure your dear parents will come looking for you."

"He is not a pony, he's a colt," Clipper corrected, showing no fear of the Troll standing before him.

"Whatever. It doesn't really matter. I have you now," Fennika said. "Archibald, take him to the castle."

Archibald stepped out from behind a tree, clapping his hands. "More little friends," he cried.

"I don't make friends with Trolls," Clipper shouted, giving Archibald's nose a pull when he leaned toward the net.

"Ouch!" Archibald cried, and thinking nose pulling was the way Nisses said hello, he grabbed Clipper's nose and gave it a tug in return. "And good-day to you, as well," he said with a bow.

As he untangled Clipper from the net, he whispered into his ear. "Don't worry little Nisse, I won't hurt you. I'm your friend."

Archibald put Clipper under his arm and headed off in the direction of the castle.

"Let me go, you big bully!" Clipper shouted, beating Archibald with his fists.

"My, my, Nisses are certainly affectionate," Archibald laughed, stepping into the woods.

The White Mare and the colt were circling the sky above the Forest of the Glen. Tandara and Balto had discovered that Clipper had fallen from the back of the colt.

"Look, Balto, below. The Trolls have captured Clipper. One of the Trolls has him under his arm," Tandara shouted.

"We have to go after him," Balto shouted, giving the White Mare a gentle nudge in her side.

On the other side of the Kingdom, Klo was pacing about in his library. He had been watching the Nisses' adventure in his fireplace.

"This is a fine kettle of fish. The Trolls have captured Clipper and Fennika has spread a net over the trees. If the White Mare swoops down to rescue Clipper, she'll be caught in the net. I have to do something."

Klo took a long thin straw from a box on the mantle. He picked a small pea off his dinner plate and put it in the end of the straw. "Now don't be upset with me, White Mare, but I have to help the Nisses."

He then pointed the straw at the fireplace and put it to his lips. He blew into the straw and the pea flew into the fireplace.

❄

Fennika was waiting impatiently in the Forest of the Glen. Finally she saw the White Mare approach in the sky.

"That's it, White Mare," she coaxed, "just a little lower and you'll be in my net."

But at that moment, the pea that Klo had shot from his peashooter came flying across the sky. It had travelled through Klo's fireplace and into the skies above the Glen. The pea struck the White Mare in her rear end. It didn't hurt, but it startled her. She swung around in the sky and headed in the opposite direction, away from the Glen, the colt following close behind her.

"Balto, the White Mare is taking us away from the Forest of the Glen!" Tandara called out.

"Something has spooked her. I can't get her to turn around. We're heading back to the Nisse Palace," Balto shouted.

"But we can't leave Clipper!" Tandara cried.

Balto thought for a moment and then replied, "I think we should go home and consult the Nisse Hand Book. As long as we have the book, Clipper will be safe. It's the Nisse Hand Book the Trolls really want."

Fennika watched as the White Mare and the colt galloped off across the sky toward the Nisse Palace. "I lost them, I lost them!" she shouted. "If I hurry, I might be able to follow the White Mare's flight in my Vat of Boiling Milk. She'll lead me to the Nisse Palace."

Fennika scurried off through the woods. But by the time she reached her castle, the White Mare had already delivered Tandara and Balto safely to the Nisse Palace. They were within its shadow by the time Fennika gazed into her Vat of Boiling Milk.

"I'm too late!" she snarled. "But there's always tomorrow. I'll have a new plan by then."

She began to yawn. The adventures of the day had tired her.

Things certainly hadn't worked out very well for Tandara and Balto, but, as they say, "it's an ill wind that blows no good." Archibald had another new friend at Troll Castle and he would take good care of Clipper and Pendulum until Balto and Tandara could rescue them.

Until tomorrow, good night.

THE TENTH DAY OF DECEMBER

Clipper had spent a comfortable night in one of the dungeons beneath Troll Castle. He was still fast asleep when Fennika unlocked the door and entered the cell.

"Well, little Nisse, I hope you slept badly," she said, shaking Clipper.

"The bed isn't very big," Clipper answered, rubbing the sleep from his eyes.

"My, my, don't we like to complain," Fennika said. "This dungeon is big enough for a little Nisse. In fact, it's big enough to hold an entire Nisse family," she added, laughing.

"You'll never catch Mama and Papa. They're too smart for you."

Fennika patted Clipper on the top of the head with her furry paws. "Oh, you're a feisty one, aren't you?"

Clipper stuck out his tongue at Fennika.

"Now listen very carefully," Fennika said. "Your parents have something I want very much. What do you suppose that is?"

"The Nisse Hand Book," Clipper said.

"Not only are you feisty, you're also clever," she said smiling. "Yes, the Nisse Hand Book. I want it very much, and I have something your parents will no doubt want to trade for it—their darling little Nisse."

"You don't scare me. As long as Mama and Papa have the Nisse Hand Book locked away in the cupboard of the Nisse Palace, you won't harm me," Clipper said.

"I wouldn't harm a darling little Nisse. Not I. But if I don't get the Nisse Hand Book, my brother Archibald may hurt you," Fennika growled.

Clipper burst out laughing. "Archibald wouldn't hurt a flea. He and Pendulum are good friends."

"Pendulum, what's a Pendulum?" Fennika asked, although she knew very well who Pendulum was.

"Archibald told me that Pendulum is in a cell down the hall," Clipper said.

"Did he?" Fennika hissed. "And I bet you'd like to see him, wouldn't you?"

"Oh yes, very much."

"If you give me those nice shiny goggles, I may take you to see him," Fennika said.

Clipper gave Fennika the goggles he had worn while he was on the back of the colt. Fennika would add them to her collection of shiny objects.

"Now take me to see my uncle," Clipper said.

"All in good time, my little darling, all in good time."

Fennika left the cell, locking the door behind her. Clipper sat on the floor. There was nothing to do but wait. He started to gather the straw from the cell. He would make some straw animals while he was waiting.

On the other side of the Kingdom, Miranda had awakened early. She wanted to visit the Christmas tree room again before she started her day's work on the Christmas Palace. She hurried along the hallway and threw open the large oak doors and stepped into the room.

She couldn't believe her eyes. The room was empty, except for one Christmas tree which stood alone in the centre of the room.

"Where did they go?" she cried.

Miranda passed by the window and spotted the Prince in the courtyard below. He was making a snowman. She threw open the windows and called to the Prince. "Your Highness, come quickly. Someone has stolen all the Christmas trees!"

The Prince looked up to the window and smiled. "No one stole the Christmas trees, Miranda," he called back.

"But there's only one left. Two days ago there were dozens in this room."

"The one that's left is the one you said was more beautiful than all the others," the Prince shouted, sticking pieces of coal in the face of the snowman.

"But what happened to all the other beautiful trees?" Miranda asked.

"I had them cut up for firewood."

"But why?"

"Because they weren't good enough. I only need one Christmas tree. I asked you to pick the best tree of the lot. The one you chose is standing in the centre of the room. I had all the other trees removed."

"But Your Highness, it's such a waste. Each one of those trees was beautiful in its own way."

The Prince laughed. "What's done is done." He returned to his snowman.

Miranda was furious. The Prince had to be taught a lesson. She leaned out the window again. "You made a mistake, Your Highness," she shouted.

"I don't make mistakes," the Prince answered, taking a bite out of the carrot he would use as the nose for the snowman.

"The tree in this room is not the one I like best," Miranda said.

"Of course it is. You told me yourself that you liked it better than all the others."

"I said no such thing. I remember telling you that, of all the trees, it was the one I least liked. You destroyed my favourite tree, after all."

"I did?" The Prince considered the situation. "Then which tree is your favourite?"

"The blue spruce," Miranda answered.

"Okay, I'll have the Foresters haul a cart of blue spruce to the Royal Palace. You can choose the best from the lot." Once again he returned to his snowman.

Miranda gathered some snow from the windowsill and rolled it into a snowball. She flung it at the Prince below and it hit him square on the top of his head, sending his crown to the ground. Miranda closed the big window and hid behind the drapes. She could hear the Prince's angry shouts bouncing off the walls of the courtyard.

"That'll teach him," she whispered, sneaking a glance out the window. The Prince was slipping and sliding in the snow, trying to pick up his crown.

I get so angry when I see him there
Head held high without a care
Laughing shouting jumping with joy
To him the world's just one big toy
It's not fair

He cheats He lies I've heard him swear
Sometimes I want to tear out my hair
Last night when I turned down my bed
*I found a frog   **Croak** it said*
Laughing shouting jumping with joy
To him the world's just one big toy
It's not fair

He says I'm cold and all too serious
His endless jokes just make me furious
He tells me I should lighten up
That from him—that whining pup
Laughing shouting jumping with joy
To him the world's just one big toy
It's not fair

Tandara and Balto had spent the entire day consulting the Nisse Hand Book. They had to find a way of getting back to Troll Castle, without the Trolls seeing them.

"Tandara, we have to hurry. It's already the tenth of December and more palaces have vanished. The Nisse Palace could be next!"

"I'm reading as fast as I can," Tandara said, not taking her eyes from the pages of the Nisse Hand Book. "I think I found something, Balto. It says here that the Trolls of the Glen use magic powders to do their mischief. They have itching powder, sneezing powder, sleeping powder and a special powder that lets them disguise themselves."

She thought about all of this for a moment, then said, "The Troll must have tricked Pendulum by disguising herself to look like one of us. Then I bet she walked right up to him."

"Does it say anything else? Does it explain how we can stay invisible long enough to search for Clipper and Pendulum? The Trolls must not see us this time."

"Yes. It says that we can remain invisible while we're away from the protection of the Nisse Palace. All we have to do is remove an empty page from the Nisse Hand Book, write our name on it, and eat it. That's the answer, Balto."

"So you mean if we each eat a page from the Nisse Hand Book, we can travel to Troll Castle and rescue Clipper and Pendulum?"

"Yes."

"There's only one problem, Tandara. If we travel on the back of the White Mare, the Trolls will set a trap like before. The pages we eat will only make *us* invisible—not the White Mare. It won't work. We'll have to find another way of getting back to the castle."

"We've solved half the problem, Balto. If we sleep on it, I'm sure we'll solve the other half after a good night's sleep."

Tandara and Balto closed the Nisse Hand Book for the night and went to bed. They had discovered a way to remain invisible while away from the Nisse Palace, but how would they travel to Troll Castle without the White Mare? Maybe the answer will come to them during the night.

Until tomorrow, good night.

THE ELEVENTH DAY OF DECEMBER

Fennika had kept her promise to Clipper. In the morning, she led Clipper into Pendulum's cell.

"You wanted to see Pendulum," she said to Clipper, "well, here he is. It'll be easier to keep an eye on both of you if you're together. But I'm warning you, don't go getting any ideas about trying to escape." Fennika glared at her prisoners. "If you do, I'll send Spike after you. He's specially trained in hunting down Nisses."

And without another word or growl, Fennika slammed the cell door and locked it behind her. She hurried upstairs to her Vat of Boiling Milk, eager to see what Balto and Tandara were up to this morning.

In the cell there was much hugging as Pendulum and his nephew were reunited.

"But where are your parents?" Pendulum asked.

"Fennika wasn't able to catch them," Clipper explained. "They probably went back to the Nisse Palace to consult the Nisse Hand Book. Uncle Pendulum, we must escape and stop the Prince."

"The Prince? What has he done?" Pendulum asked. He was still thinking about Balto and Tandara.

"The Prince is making all the palaces in the Kingdom disappear—one after another. He has a Magic Compass the wizard made for him."

"A Magic Compass?"

"Yes. Papa and Mama say if we can borrow the Compass, you'll be able to fix its magic powers so the Nisse Palace won't vanish."

"Well that would explain it," Pendulum said, brightening. "I wondered why all the palaces were vanishing in front of my eyes! But why does the Prince want the palaces to disappear?"

"He wants to build a Christmas Palace," Clipper said. "He thinks all the other palaces are old and not very interesting. And now Fennika wants to find the Nisse Palace and steal the Nisse Hand Book," Clipper added.

Pendulum was suddenly hungry. This was a lot of information to absorb on an empty stomach. "I must think of a plan," he said. "But thinking makes me hungry. I haven't had breakfast."

"Try some of this soup," Clipper said, "Archibald made it."

Pendulum made a face and took a spoonful of the cold soup. "I don't know how we're ever going to escape from this dungeon," he said.

"Maybe Archibald will help us," Clipper said. "Poor Archibald. He's the loneliest Troll I've ever met. I'm sure he'd love to help us, but he's afraid of his sister." Then Clipper looked at his uncle. "I guess I didn't do too well trying to rescue you, did I?"

"You were very brave. Don't worry, your Mama and Papa will find an answer to our troubles in the pages of the Nisse Hand Book."

Across the Kingdom in the Royal Palace, Klo was eating lunch with Miranda. "Are you still upset with the Prince about the Christmas trees?" he asked.

"Yes. I saw the Forester arrive this morning with cartloads of blue spruce. The staff is decorating them now," Miranda said.

"And the Prince wants you to choose one over all the others, I suppose."

"Exactly. Then he'll have the rest of the trees cut into firewood. He's only interested in the best, and the best can only be one tree or one palace. It's a good thing I don't have a twin sister, Uncle Klo. Otherwise the Prince would make one of us vanish," Miranda said.

Klo began to laugh. "What a thought. Imagine, two Mirandas. I don't think the Prince would be able to handle two of you."

The clock struck the hour and Klo folded his napkin. "Miranda, lunch is over. I have some thinking to do. You should go to your quarters and read blueprints, or whatever it is you architects do."

Klo took his niece by the elbow and guided her to the door. "Guards, open up!"

The doors opened and Klo gently pushed Miranda into the corridor.

"But I haven't had dessert," Miranda protested.

"You can have two tomorrow."

"But Uncle, -"

But the guards shut the doors before she could finish her sentence. Klo crossed the room, still chuckling. "Imagine, two Mirandas."

He passed his hand over one of the books on the bookshelf beside the fireplace and the wall slid open, revealing a secret passage. Klo lit a torch and walked along the passage. He came to a set of stairs at the end of the hallway. He made his way quickly down the staircase and entered his laboratory, lighting other torches along the way.

The room was filled with everything that a good wizard would ever need. There were jars brimming with herbs and medicines, the stone walls were covered with charts of the heavens. The tables were littered with scrolls. In the corner was a large fireplace.

He threw a few extra logs on the fire to warm up the room. Then he ground some herbs into a pot of water to make tea and set the pot over the roaring fire. The mice that lived in the laboratory scurried across the shelves.

"My little friends, I suppose you're hungry," Klo said, and crumbled some bread between his fingers and scattered it in the corner. Klo always fed the mice because their tails brushed away the dust from his books. It saved him the trouble of having to dust them himself.

In the centre of the room, on a high pedestal, stood the most important book in Klo's collection. It was his Book of Charms. Klo put on his reading spectacles and slowly began to turn the pages in the great book.

"I may have lost my power over the Prince, but there is nothing to stop me from looking for a good charm to help the Nisses. Time is running out and I must be prepared to help them when the Prince pardons me. That is, *if* he pardons me."

Klo blew the dust off the pages as he continued to read. He studied his Book of Charms for the rest of that afternoon and evening, resting only to sip his wizard's tea or to throw a fresh log on the fire.

As evening approached, Tandara and Balto once again stood in the burrows that ran beneath the Nisse Palace.

Balto had torn several blank pages from the Nisse Hand Book. He and Tandara had each signed their name to a page. Balto tucked the other pages safely into his pocket. "That should do the trick," he said. "If we meet the Trolls, they won't be able to see us because we're invisible."

"We still don't know how to find Troll Castle," Tandara said. "There are hundreds of burrows down here and we aren't even sure there is a path that leads to the Glen."

She began to tremble. "Goodness, that wind is cold," she said, rubbing her shoulders.

"That's it!" Balto shouted. "That's the answer!"

"Balto, what are you babbling about?"

"We'll follow the wind," he said. "All the cold winds in the Kingdom come from the Glen."

"Of course," Tandara said. "It makes sense. If we follow the wind, we'll find the Trolls."

Balto stuck one finger into his mouth, then held it up to the air, testing for the direction of the cold wind. "This way," he said, "we're on our way."

And off they went, following the cold wind through the burrows.

Archibald waited until Fennika fell asleep before he crept into the kitchen of the castle. He carefully removed the tiny Christmas tree from the cupboard and placed it on the table. It had drooped to the side again and Archibald gave it a drink of water from Spike's bowl.

The little tree shuddered and stretched until it stood tall in its pot.

"Spike, I think our little tree has grown since yesterday."

Spike arched his head to the side to get a better view of the little tree and began

Archibald in the forest, wishing upon shooting stars

to wag his tail.

"It's time for your walk," Archibald said.

He tucked the little Christmas tree under his arm and opened the door that led outside. Spike scampered along beside him. The air was crisp and stars filled the sky, twinkling and sparkling over the Kingdom. Archibald came to a clearing in the forest and scooped some earth to the side. He placed the little tree in the ground and packed dirt around it.

"Look, Spike," Archibald shouted, pointing to the sky, "a shooting star!" They both gazed at the sky and watched as the pink tail crossed the heavens.

"I better make a wish," Archibald said, closing his eyes. "I wish that my little Christmas tree will grow strong and tall."

Spike gave a little bark and Archibald opened his eyes as the sky exploded into colour. "The sky is filled with shooting stars!" Archibald shouted.

He lay back on the snow. "A sky full of shooting stars means a sky full of wishes."

Archibald began to point at the shooting stars as they danced across the night sky. "I wish that Fennika will free Pendulum and Clipper," he said to one. "I wish the Nisses will take me to the Nisse Palace," he said, pointing to another. "And I wish to celebrate Christmas with all my new friends and all my old friends." He patted Spike on the head. "I'm going to keep my eyes open all night and make a wish on every shooting star I see," Archibald said, yawning.

But after only a few minutes, he was fast asleep with Spike curled beside him. And as he slept, the little Christmas tree, nourished on the power of moon beams and good wishes, grew another foot. And slowly as the evening wore on, the stars turned out their lights and went to bed.

Until tomorrow, good night.

THE TWELFTH DAY OF DECEMBER

The carpenters and masons were busy at work on the Christmas Palace. Miranda inspected the quality of the stone that would support the walls of the west wing while she supervised the mixing of the cement for the east wing. And there were over twenty varieties of bricks—among them, a red brick for the chimneys, a soft brick for the fireplaces, a rose brick for the soup kitchen hearths and a chalk brick for the Bakers' ovens.

The carpenters asked her opinion on the pine wood to be laid in the north wing and the masons wanted to know if the polish on the marble was smooth enough for the tiles in the south wing. And there were plenty of disagreements between the masons and carpenters that she also had to settle.

The Prince arrived in his Royal Sleigh and approached his tired architect. "Miranda, I trust everything is on schedule."

The Prince was the last person Miranda wanted to see today. The truth was, everything was not on schedule. There had been several delays. "Yes, Your Highness. Well, almost," she muttered.

"I looked over your reports last night, and I've made a few minor adjustments," the Prince said.

"Adjustments?"

The Prince had been supplying her with adjustments every day. This was the reason there were so many delays.

The Prince snapped his fingers and four of his valets approached. Their arms were laden with blueprints which they passed to Miranda. There wasn't room in her arms for the last blueprint so the valet placed it in her mouth.

"These are the new changes, Miranda."

Miranda began to mumble but the Prince couldn't understand what she was saying.

"What was that you said?" The Prince asked, removing the blueprint from her mouth.

"I said this is unfair, you can't keep making changes every single day. The palace will never be finished by Christmas if you keep bothering me with twaddle. I've a good mind to..."

But the Prince had heard enough. He smiled and stuck the blueprint back into Miranda's mouth, cutting her off. He laughed and climbed back into the sleigh.

"Keep up the good work, Miranda," he called as he drove away.

Miranda spit the blueprint from her mouth and threw the others to the ground. "I can't make any more decisions today."

At Troll Castle, Archibald was finishing a game of checkers with Clipper.

"I beat you again, Archibald," Clipper said.

"Only because I let you win," Archibald answered, and they both laughed.

Clipper threw his arms around Archibald's shoulders and gave him a big hug. "You may be a Troll, Archibald, but you're the nicest Troll I've ever met."

Archibald began to cry.

"What is it, Archibald?" Clipper asked. "Did I upset you?"

Archibald wiped the tears from his eyes. "No, no. It's just that I'm so happy. These last days together with you and Pendulum have been the happiest of my life."

"Papa says that Trolls are always grumpy like Fennika. But you're different, Archibald. You have a good side too," Clipper said, giving him another hug.

Pendulum, who had been watching their game, agreed. "Yes, indeed, Clipper. Trolls have a good side too."

Pendulum
Trolls have eyes that see at night
They even sparkle at day's first light
They brush their fur from foot to head
Sometimes they even make their bed
Trolls have a good side too

Archibald
But Trolls are rotten to the core
Closing windows and slamming doors
Fresh air makes them sniff and sneeze
Whoever heard a Troll say please

Pendulum
Some Trolls make lifelong friendships
Just ask Spike about our kinship

Spike
Woof

Archibald cleared his throat. "I have an announcement to make."

The Nisses waited.

"I've decided to set you free."

"But what about Fennika?" Pendulum asked. "She'll be very cross with you." Even though he wanted to be free, Pendulum didn't want to see Archibald get into trouble with Fennika.

"This is my castle, too," Archibald said defiantly. "Now follow me before I change my mind."

He put his key into the lock of the cell door. The Nisses looked over his shoulder and watched him fumble with the key. Suddenly a shadow fell over them and they all looked up slowly. There stood Fennika standing on the other side of the door.

"And where do you think you're going?" she demanded.

"I was just taking the Nisses for a walk," Archibald said, his knees trembling.

"If you like your little friends so much Archibald, then you can stay here with them."

"Do you mean that?" Archibald asked, excited.

"She means that you are now a prisoner like us," Pendulum said.

"Exactly, and I want no more trouble from any of you. I'm getting impatient. I want the Nisse Hand Book and I want it soon!" Fennika said, shaking her paw at the Nisses. "I'm going upstairs to look into my Vat of Boiling Milk. Those other Nisses must be on their way back here by now."

The Nisses were silent, which made Fennika more angry.

"Or maybe they're planning something," she said, more to herself. "Well, let them try. I'll be prepared. I have nets set at all the entrances of the castle, even over the windows. If they try to get in—snap! Caught like a fly in a spider's web. Fennika's web that is," she said, snickering. "Now give me your key, Archibald."

He passed Fennika the key through the bars. She slipped it into the hole on the outside of the door, beyond their reach, and headed upstairs.

Tandara and Balto had finally arrived at the end of the long burrow. They stood in front of a stone wall.

"I think Troll Castle is on the other side," Balto said. "But how do we get through?"

Tandara began to press on the stones. "This one is loose," she said and pushed her weight against it. The stone fell to the floor on the other side.

"We'd better eat another page of the Nisse Hand Book to make sure we're still invisible," Tandara suggested.

They quickly scribbled their names on new pages and popped them into their mouths. They crawled through the opening, replacing the stone in the wall when they were safely on the other side.

"It looks like a dungeon," Tandara whispered.

Carefully making their way along the damp, dark corridor, passing empty cell after empty cell, they finally heard familiar voices drift toward them. At the end of the corridor, in the very last cell, their search ended.

"Clipper, Pendulum, we found you!" Tandara cried. She turned the key in the lock and swung open the door of the cell.

"Mama, Papa!" Clipper shouted, rushing to his parents.

"We thought you would never find us," Pendulum said, giving his brother a big hug. "How did you do it?"

"There's no time to explain," Balto said. "We have to leave right away."

But in their excitement, Tandara and Balto had closed the door behind them and left the key in the lock outside. The door couldn't be opened from the inside.

"Oh no," Tandara whispered, "what are we going to do?"

Balto scratched his head and turned to his brother Pendulum. "When does the Troll feed you?"

"In the morning."

"Then, when the Troll comes and opens the door, we'll slip outside," Balto said.

"But she'll see you," Clipper said.

"The Trolls can't see us. We ate a page from the Nisse Hand Book. We're invisible to them," Balto explained.

"Of course, I'd forgotten about that trick," Pendulum said.

"In the meantime," Tandara suggested, "we might as well relax and get a good night's sleep. The important thing is that we are together now."

At that moment Archibald woke up. He had been taking a nap in the corner.

"A Troll!" Tandara shouted.

"It's only Archibald," Clipper said. "He won't hurt us, he's our friend."

"A Troll? A friend? I never heard of such a thing," Balto protested.

"Archibald is a very special Troll," Pendulum explained. "His sister Fennika is the nasty Troll. Archibald was trying to help us escape but Fennika caught him and put him here in the cell with us."

Archibald rubbed his eyes. "Who are you talking to?"

"Archibald, I would like to introduce you to the other Nisses who live at the Nisse Palace," Pendulum said.

Archibald looked around but he couldn't see anyone other than Clipper and Pendulum.

"You can't see us because we're invisible," Balto said.

"Are you sure our new guests are invisible? I can't see them," Archibald said.

"That's what invisible means," Clipper explained, laughing.

"If you say so. It's very nice to meet you, Nisses from the Nisse Palace, wherever you are," Archibald said, bowing.

"I have a surprise for everyone," Tandara said, removing a big bowl from her knapsack.

"Rice Pudding!" Clipper shouted.

"I may not be able to see our new guests, but I can smell something good,"

Archibald said. "Rice Pudding? Is it true? I've never eaten Rice Pudding."

"There's enough for everyone—even for a Troll," Tandara said. "I'll put it over here in the corner for you, Archibald. Once it's away from us, the magic will wear off and you can see it. Now eat up, we have to get a good night's sleep."

The Nisses are reunited once again. Will Balto and Tandara be able to slip out of the cell when Fennika comes to feed them in the morning? And will Miranda be able to keep up with all the Prince's changes to the Christmas Palace?

Until tomorrow, good night.

THE THIRTEENTH DAY OF DECEMBER

Miranda found the Prince on the ski slope close to the Royal Palace. She stood impatiently at the bottom and watched as the Prince skilfully wound his way down the hill, picking up speed as he went along. He came to a halt at her feet, spraying fresh snow over her boots.

"Miranda, I was looking for you earlier," he said, taking off his goggles.

"Yes, I know," she replied, "I got your Royal Summons."

"Why don't you grab a pair of skis and come with me?" he said. "The weather is perfect and the snow couldn't be better."

"Is that the only reason you called me away from my work?"

"Sure, you know what they say about all work and no play."

"That's easy for you to say, Your Highness," Miranda snapped. "You don't have to get up at the crack of dawn every morning to go to work." She spun on her heel and started to walk away.

"By the way, Miranda, I had the Foresters deliver and decorate the blue spruce."

Miranda faced the Prince once again. "Blue spruce? What are you talking about?"

"The Christmas tree room. Remember? You were upset because I destroyed the blue spruce. Now you have an entire room of blue spruce."

"But, Your Highness, you've made a mistake. It was the red spruce that caught my eye," Miranda said, with the trace of a smile.

"No, it wasn't. I distinctly remember—your favourite Christmas tree is the blue spruce."

"His Highness should have his ears cleaned. I like red spruce, not blue spruce."

Miranda turned again but her boot caught the tip of one of his skis and she fell into the snow. The Prince reached down and pulled her to her feet.

"Thank you," Miranda muttered, but she lost her footing again, this time falling toward the Prince, knocking him to the ground. She landed on top of him.

"I'm sorry, Your Highness," Miranda said, as they stood again, looking around on the ground. "I lost my mittens."

"I'll warm your hands, Miranda," the Prince offered, taking her hands between his own and rubbing her fingers.

"Close your eyes," he said.

Miranda closed her eyes and enjoyed the massage as the heat returned to her fingers. The Prince gently raised her hands to his lips and kissed her fingertips. Then, the Prince kissed Miranda on the lips.

"How dare you!" Miranda shouted, opening her eyes. "How dare you kiss me!"

Meanwhile, on the far side of the Kingdom, the Nisses in the dungeons of Troll Castle were waiting patiently for Fennika to arrive with breakfast.

"Now remember, Archibald, don't say a word to Fennika about Mama and Papa," Clipper warned.

"She wouldn't believe me, anyway," Archibald replied. "If I told her there were two more Nisses in here that she couldn't see, she'd say I was playing with imaginary friends again."

Suddenly they heard Fennika's shuffling footsteps coming down the corridor.

"She's coming," Pendulum whispered. "Now stand on either side of the door. When she opens it, rush out and don't bump into her."

Tandara and Balto stood on opposite sides of the cell door. Fennika came around the corner carrying a tray.

"So, my little darling prisoners," she said as she approached the door, "I've brought you some cold soup."

The Nisses eagerly waited for her to open the door of the cell. But Fennika disappointed them. Instead, she slid the tray under the bars and into the cell.

"Well, don't just stand there, take the tray," she ordered.

Pendulum took the tray from Fennika, and without another word she spun on her tail and left. When she was safely out of earshot, Tandara and Balto moved away from the door.

"Our plan didn't work," Tandara said.

"We'll have to wait until tomorrow and try again," Pendulum said with a sigh. "She only visits us once a day."

"Let's hope she comes into the cell tomorrow," Balto added.

"Until then, we might as well eat to keep up our spirits," Tandara said. "It's a good thing I packed lots of Rice Pudding."

Later that evening, Miranda decided to pay a visit to Klo. She was still upset with the Prince. "The nerve of him, kissing me," she thought, touching her fingers to her lips. The memory of the kiss began to make her anger fade. "The Prince never kissed me before," she whispered.

The guards let her into Klo's library.

"Uncle Klo, where are you?" she asked, looking around.

But Klo was nowhere to be found.

"He must be in his laboratory." She crossed the room to the bookcase. "Now let's see, which book is it?"

Miranda began to pull on the bindings of several books. After her tenth try, the secret panel slid open. "I'll just check in on Uncle Klo, but I won't disturb him," she thought.

She walked down the corridor and came to the top of the staircase and looked down into the laboratory below. Klo was sound asleep in his chair, close to the pedestal which held his Book of Charms. Miranda smiled. "Just as I thought, he's up to his old tricks," she whispered. "I better not let him catch me here."

She retraced her steps to the library, closing the secret panel behind her.

Klo awoke and rubbed his eyes, glancing at his stopwatch. "Now where was I?" he said, gathering his thoughts. "Yes, I was looking for a way to free the Nisses from the Trolls. I wish I had never given the Prince that Magic Compass. The Nisses wouldn't be in all this trouble if it weren't for me. If I could just find the right spell." He went back to reading from his Book of Charms.

Blade of fennel   Hair of cat
Ring of onion   Wing of bat
Juice of stone and tail of rat
A little this   A little that

No no no
It won't do
I'm no wizard   Just a fool

But of course—

Juice of stone   Wing of bat
Blade of fennel   Tail of rat
Ring of onion and hair of cat
A little this   A little that

No no no
It won't do
I'm no wizard   Just a fool

But of course—

Mix it once   In this hat
Quill of feather   Ounce of fat
Wipe my feet   On the mat
A little this   A little that

No no no
It won't do
I'm no wizard   Just a fool

The Wizard, Klo, reading from his Book of Charms

But of course—

Wipe my feet   Ounce of fat
Mix it once   On the mat
Quill of feather   In this hat
A little this   A little that

No no no
It won't do

Klo closed the Book of Charms. "I'll just have to read more tomorrow and hope the Nisses can help themselves until I figure something out."

He glanced at his watch again. "It'll soon be time for bed," he said, and wearily climbed the stairs back to his library.

Would Klo be able to find the right spell to help the Nisses? And would the Nisses be able to trick Fennika tomorrow and slip out of the dungeon?

Until tomorrow, good night.

THE FOURTEENTH DAY OF DECEMBER

Miranda and Klo were enjoying a leisurely breakfast.

"Uncle Klo, why were you in your laboratory yesterday?"

"Have you been spying on me?" Klo asked, arching his eyebrow.

"Of course not, I came to visit you yesterday and you weren't here. I just guessed that you were in your laboratory," she explained, not mentioning that she actually had gone down there.

"I was reading my Book of Charms," Klo said, sipping his tea.

"But you told me that as long as the Prince has you under house arrest, you're not allowed to leave your chambers."

"Yes, that's true," Klo answered, smiling.

"Then you've broken the law."

"My secret laboratory is part of my chambers, so I haven't disobeyed the Prince."

"But the Prince doesn't know you have a secret laboratory," Miranda said.

"Yes, and what the Prince doesn't know won't hurt him."

"Then you can use your magic after all," Miranda said with a grin.

"Yes and no. The magic that's available to me while I'm a prisoner is limited. I have no power over the Prince or the Magic Compass. I can do nothing to make him change his mind about making the palaces disappear. But I can try to help the Nisses."

Miranda began to laugh. "Uncle Klo, I told you already, I'm too old to believe in fairy tales."

Klo said nothing. He crossed the room to the bookcase and opened the secret panel in the wall. "Come with me, Miranda, I want to show you something."

Miranda followed her uncle. It was the first time he had ever invited her to his laboratory.

Deep within the dungeons of Troll Castle, the Nisses were waiting for Fennika to arrive again with breakfast.

"Pendulum, make sure that Fennika opens the door to the cell this time," Balto said.

"I'll do my best," Pendulum promised.

"As soon as we're free, we'll all hurry back to the safety of the Nisse Palace," Tandara said.

"I'm afraid we won't be able to leave the castle right away," Pendulum remarked.

"What do you mean?" Balto asked.

"Fennika has stolen my oiling can. I won't be able to stop the magic of the Compass without my oiling can—it's my most important tinkering tool."

"Do you know where it is?" Tandara asked.

"I know where it is," Archibald said, facing Tandara. Although he couldn't see Tandara or Balto, he knew where they were by their voices.

"Fennika keeps all her shiny toys in the cupboards of the kitchen," he said.

Suddenly Clipper whispered, "I can hear Fennika."

Tandara and Balto took up their positions on either side of the cell door.

"Here's your breakfast," Fennika growled, shoving the tray under the door.

Spike began to bark.

"Make that dog stop yapping!" Fennika ordered. "It gives me a headache."

"I think Spike needs to go for a walk, Fennika," Pendulum said. "He's been cooped up here for a couple of days."

"Well, another hour or two isn't going to make any difference."

"But his barks will get louder and you'll get a bigger headache," Pendulum said.

"I suppose you've got a point," Fennika said. She unlocked the cell and Spike scampered toward her, jumping up and licking her face. "Get this mutt off me!" she cried.

While Spike was busy distracting Fennika, Tandara and Balto slipped out of the cell.

Fennika managed to get Spike under control and slammed the cell door. Spike took off ahead of her down the halls. "Come back here," she called after him, but Spike disappeared around the corner. "Heel boy, heel," she shouted, following him.

"It worked!" Clipper cried when he was sure Fennika was gone.

"Spike was very clever to think of that trick," Pendulum said.

"As soon as we find the oiling can, we'll come back and free you," Balto said from the other side of the door.

Pendulum wished Balto and Tandara luck as they set out to find the kitchen.

As Balto and Tandara were searching for Pendulum's oiling can, Klo was leading Miranda down the stairs to his secret laboratory in the Royal Palace. He piled several logs in the fireplace as Miranda looked over his collection of magic.

"Don't touch anything," Klo warned, "much of what I have is very fragile."

"I'm just looking," Miranda said.

"Now Miranda, we're going to have a little talk about the Nisses," Klo said.

Spike licking Fennika's face

"Again?" Miranda said, laughing.

"Miranda, you must listen to what I'm going to tell you."

But Miranda was only half listening. She was fascinated by all the jars and scrolls in the laboratory. "Brrr. It's cold down here. Can you light a fire?" she asked, rubbing her shoulders.

"You seem to have mastered the magic required to build a fire, Miranda. I was very impressed with the roaring fire you created in my library. Go ahead, try it again," Klo said, stepping away from the fireplace.

"But Uncle Klo, I've never actually started a fire with magic. The fire in your library was already burning, I just helped it along."

"Then now is as good a time as any to improve your powers. Come here. Stand in front of the hearth."

Miranda slowly approached the great stone fireplace and stood in front of the logs. Klo stood behind her and gently held her shoulders. "Now concentrate," he whispered in her ear, "start a fire with the logs."

Miranda stared at the logs and knitted her brows, concentrating. But the logs wouldn't light. "I don't have the power," Miranda said.

"We'll try again. First you must believe in what you do. Are you ready?"

Miranda nodded and stared again at the logs. She concentrated so hard her body trembled. But still no fire. "I can't do it!"

"Yes, you can. Clear your thoughts and think only of the fire. Imagine the logs bursting into flames. Try," Klo whispered, urging her on.

Miranda relaxed and took a deep breath. "I want a big fire!" she shouted.

No sooner had she spoken when the logs exploded into flames. Miranda was so stunned by what she had done, she fell backward. Klo caught her. "I did it, Uncle Klo. I did it!"

"Yes, but now you have to control it or it'll burn down the whole palace," Klo said, proud of his niece.

Miranda gently blew on the logs and the fire settled in the hearth. "There, everything's under control," Miranda whispered, still amazed at what she had accomplished.

"This is only the beginning, Miranda," Klo said.

"The beginning, Uncle Klo? I don't understand."

"What do you see when you look into the fire?"

"I see the flames."

"What else? What else do you see when you look deep into the fire?"

Miranda followed the flames with her eyes as they danced in the fireplace. She looked deep into the fire. "I think I see something," she said, looking even deeper.

And within the glow of the fire Miranda saw Tandara and Balto appear in the flames. They were standing in the kitchen of Troll Castle, looking through the cupboards. Miranda saw them as clearly as though she were there. "I see the Nisses, Uncle Klo. They look just as you described them to me in the fairy tales."

And as she considered this thought, the image in the fireplace faded from sight and the flames died down. "What happened? Where did they go?" Miranda asked, blinking to clear her vision.

"It takes much practice to hold the magic, Miranda. But I'm impressed that you were able to hold the image as long as you did. Bravo."

Miranda was still staring at the fireplace. "Can I try one of the spells from your Book of Charms to bring them back?"

Klo crossed the room and sat in his chair. "No, Miranda. My Book of Charms is very powerful. You would have to be an experienced wizard like me to use the book."

"What was that strange place I saw?" Miranda asked. "Why have I never seen the Nisses before?"

"You've never seen the Nisses because you've never tried."

Miranda sat beside Klo. "But I just saw them. So they must be real."

Klo began to tell Miranda everything that had happened to the Nisses since the first of December.

Tandara and Balto had found Pendulum's oiling can in the kitchen where Archibald had said it would be. They rushed back to the dungeons and opened the door of the cell.

"We'd better hurry," Balto said to the others, "Fennika will probably come back soon."

They all rushed to the end of the hallway. Balto found the loose stone and gave it a push. It fell to the ground on the other side of the tunnel.

"Your mother and I will go through first," Balto said to Clipper, "then you and Pendulum can follow."

"What about me?" Archibald asked.

Everyone turned to look at him. They had forgotten all about the Troll.

"Mama, Papa, we can't leave Archibald here," Clipper said.

"We can't take the Troll with us," Balto said.

"But he's been so good to us. It's our fault he's here in the cell with us," Clipper said.

"That's true, but..." Balto wasn't sure what to do.

"Please, don't leave me here," Archibald pleaded. "Fennika will be very angry with me when she discovers you've all escaped."

"Well, all right," Balto said. "But hurry."

The Nisses and Archibald crawled through the opening in the wall and when they were safe within the burrow on the other side, Balto replaced the stone. "This way," he said, "it's a long walk. We'll stop and spend the night at the White Palace."

Archibald followed the Nisses, his heart pounding with excitement. He was on his way to the Nisse Palace and new adventures.

Until tomorrow, good night.

THE FIFTEENTH DAY OF DECEMBER

After a long journey through the burrows, Archibald and the Nisses finally arrived at the White Palace, Pendulum's home.

Archibald and Clipper admired the many fine clocks in Pendulum's workshop as Tandara and Balto prepared Rice Pudding. Pendulum was polishing his trusted oiling can with a cloth.

"I haven't had guests here at the White Palace for a long time," he said happily.

"Can I help you stir the Rice Pudding, Tandara?" Archibald asked.

"Certainly, Archibald," she answered, passing him the spoon.

Suddenly his eyes were the size of saucers. "I can see you, Tandara, I can see you!" he shouted, turning to Balto. "And I can see you too, Balto."

"The magic has worn off," Tandara said. "We're no longer invisible."

"What a relief! Now Archibald won't be bumping into me all the time or stepping on my feet," Balto said smiling as he rubbed his aching foot.

"As soon as we're finished eating, we should continue on to the Nisse Palace," Pendulum suggested. "Fennika must surely have discovered us missing by now. We won't be safe here at the White Palace for very long."

"Will I be able to live with you at the Nisse Palace?" Archibald asked.

"Of course," Tandara said, giving Archibald a hug.

"Did you hear that, Spike? We're going to live at the Nisse Palace," Archibald said, stuffing his mouth with a spoonful of Rice Pudding.

But Spike wasn't there. He was back at Troll Castle, with Fennika.

"Oh, Archibald," Clipper said, "we forgot Spike."

"Fennika doesn't like Spike," Archibald said. "And Spike is my friend. I can't go to the Nisse Palace without my best friend."

"But Archibald, we can't turn back now," Pendulum said.

"I have to go back and get him," Archibald said, looking from one face to another. "I can't leave Spike, he's my friend."

One friend sure is better than none
Spike always doubles my fun
Candy tastes better when you're two

74

So keep a piece in your shoe
Spike can always make me smile
When I'm sad every once in awhile

❅

While Archibald was worrying about his good friend Spike, the Prince was waiting for Miranda in the Great Hall of the Royal Palace. It was filled with red spruce trees. He was pacing back and forth because Miranda was late for their meeting.

Finally she entered the Great Hall and ignored the room full of trees.

"Miranda, where have you been? You were supposed to meet me here yesterday," the Prince said.

"I'm sorry, Your Majesty. I've been…ill the last few days. Yes," she repeated. "I've been ill," and she began to cough.

She didn't want to tell the Prince she had spent the night in Klo's secret laboratory, listening to stories about the adventures of the Nisses.

"Ill? Why didn't you send me a note? I hope you're feeling better," the Prince said, concerned.

"Yes, thank you."

"Then we'd better drive out to the construction site and make up for lost time. The palace must be finished by Christmas Day."

But Miranda had planned to spend the rest of the day with Klo. She wanted to help him find a spell from his Book of Charms so they could help the Nisses.

"I'm sorry, Your Highness, I can't go out there today," she said. "I think I've still got the flu." She coughed another unconvincing cough.

"Why do I get the feeling you're keeping something from me?" the Prince asked, circling Miranda.

"Oh, all right," she confessed. "I never was very good at telling lies. I've been spending time with my uncle. But don't ask me anything else. I can't tell you more because you won't believe me."

"Try me," the Prince said, crossing his arms. "And that's a Royal Command."

Miranda hesitated, but knew better than to refuse. "If you insist. Uncle Klo and I have been awake all night trying to find a way to help the Nisses," Miranda said.

The Prince began to laugh. "You mean Klo has been entertaining you with fairy tales? I thought you were too old for make-believe, Miranda."

"I knew you wouldn't believe me. This is all your fault. You've placed the Nisses in great danger by making the palaces disappear," Miranda said. "And I don't have time to waste trying to change your mind." She started for the door.

"But Miranda," the Prince called, running to the doorway, "You didn't even notice the red spruce trees."

"It's obvious you've made another mistake. I told you my favourite Christmas tree was the white spruce," she said, disappearing around the corner.

The Prince shook his head in defeat and went back to the Great Hall. He sat on the windowsill and watched the snowflakes as they fell outside. "I've had enough. Miranda is planning to sabotage my Christmas Palace. She and Klo are trying to keep me from finishing it. And all this talk about Nisses. What do they think I am, a child?"

He took the Magic Compass from his pocket. "I'll show them." he said, opening the Compass. He pointed the needle over the White Palace on the dial and with a smirk snapped the Compass shut.

He opened the Compass again. With a quick twist of his wrist, he set the needle in motion so that it would run on its own. From now on, the Magic Compass would make one palace in the Kingdom disappear every day.

At that moment, Fennika was balancing a tray of soup as she entered the dungeons of Troll Castle. Spike followed, nipping at her heels. "Stop biting me," Fennika growled, "or I'll make you into dog soup."

She turned the corner to find the cell door wide open and her prisoners gone. She threw the tray to the floor and poked her nose into the cell. "They're gone, and Archibald with them!" she bellowed. "When I catch him, I'm going to make him into soup too!" She shook her paw at the empty cell.

"I don't know how they did it, but I know how I can follow them. One of my magic powders will do the trick."

Soon after Fennika discovered her prisoners had escaped, Archibald and the Nisses were standing in the courtyard of the White Palace. Tandara passed Archibald the lunch she had packed for his trip.

"Are you sure you want to go back to Troll Castle, Archibald?" Clipper asked.

"Yes, I have to help Spike."

"Are you sure you can find your way home?" Pendulum asked.

"Yes. It's a day's travel through the forest in the direction of the cold wind."

"Why don't you return through the burrow?" Balto asked.

"This is probably the only chance I'll ever get to see the Kingdom. I want to see the trees, feel snow under my paws, and listen to the birds. Until now, I've only dreamt about them. We don't have these things in the Glen."

Tandara dabbed the tears at the corner of her eyes with her hanky. "We'll miss you, Archibald," she said, blowing her nose.

Archibald gave his new friends a big Troll hug and entered the forest. The Nisses continued waving until Archibald disappeared among the trees. When they turned to go back inside the White Palace, they discovered that it was no longer there. It had vanished.

"Oh no, the White Palace is gone!" Pendulum cried. "The Prince used that Magic Compass to make my home vanish."

"Then we must continue our journey through the burrows to the Nisse Palace," Balto said. "It's a good thing your oiling can didn't vanish too."

"Oh, Pendulum," Tandara said, "all your beautiful clocks are gone forever."

"Wait until I get my hands on that Magic Compass," Pendulum growled, "I'll fix it."

"Then we'd better hurry," Balto said, "the Nisse Palace may be next."

The Nisses took one last look at the spot where the White Palace once stood.

"Gone," Pendulum thought, "and with it the mechanical toy I made for Clipper."

Silently the Nisses entered the burrow and continued their journey homeward to the Nisse Palace.

But the Nisses were not the only travellers this day.

In the dungeons of Troll Castle, Fennika peeked into the powder pouch she had packed for her own trip. "I have all my magic powders with me," she said. "And this is the one that will help me now!"

She held the canister up to the light: **NISSE FOOT POWDER**

"Just what I need," she mumbled and sprinkled the powder on the floor. Suddenly the footprints of all the Nisses appeared. "Excellent," Fennika shouted, shaking more powder onto the floor.

She followed the footprints until she came to the stone wall. Quickly she found the loose stone and pushed on it. It fell to the floor on the other side of the burrow. Fennika stepped through the hole and replaced the stone.

"All I have to do is follow the footprints, and before you know it, I'll be at the Nisse Palace. And then I'll find the Nisse Hand Book," she said, letting out a loud Troll laugh which echoed through the burrows.

Spike had been left alone at Troll Castle. He could hear Fennika's laughter as it faded down the burrow. There was nothing else for him to do but wait. He spied the tray of soup that Fennika had dropped and he eagerly lapped it up from the floor. At least he wouldn't be hungry. He lay down and curled himself into a ball to wait for the return of his good friend, Archibald.

Would Fennika's magic powders lead her to the Nisses? And would Archibald be able to find his way back to Troll Castle to rescue his friend Spike?

Until tomorrow, good night.

THE SIXTEENTH DAY OF DECEMBER

The birds woke Archibald from his sleep in the forest. He crawled out from under the roots of a tree that he had discovered on his journey back to the Glen.

"Good morning little birds," he said.

A rabbit hopped out from under a log and scampered through the brush, her white fur coat blending in with the snow. A pair of winter pigeons began to coo in the trees above Archibald's head.

"I could stay here forever," he sighed.

He had never seen the creatures of the forest before. As he continued exploring, he came to a brook that had frozen over except for a thin stream in the middle.

"What strange glass," he thought, seeing his reflection in the ice below.

He had never seen a frozen brook before. As he bent over to admire his reflection, he lost his balance and tumbled off the bank onto the ice. Down, down the brook he slid, his arms and feet waving in the frosty air. "Wheeeeeee!" Archibald cried. It was the most fun he'd ever had!

Archibald thundered along on his stomach, faster and faster. Suddenly, the brook took a sharp turn and Archibald flew off the ice and into a snowbank. He sat up and shook the snow from his fur, a little dizzy from his trip down the brook.

"What an adventure!" he shouted up to the sky.

He looked around in surprise. "I can't believe my eyes," he said, slowly rising to his feet. He was in the middle of the Prince's Christmas tree forest. There were hundreds and hundreds of trees. "This must be paradise," he thought, as he admired the spruce, pine, and fir trees that surrounded him." This is a perfect spot to eat breakfast."

He sat in the middle of the Christmas tree forest to unpack the lunch Tandara had prepared for him.

In a forest   In a glen
In a field   Or fox's den
There grows a seed
A little each day
Bursting forth on the first of May

Through rains of Spring
And Summer's warmth
Under Autumn's cloak
And wind from North
The little seed grows strong and tall

Archibald sliding on the frozen brook

Until that day
It decks the hall

Balls of glass
Sparkle on green
Presents wrapped with all our dreams
Candy canes dangle
And strings of berries
Adorn your figure
To make us merry

Archibald spent the rest of the morning admiring the trees. Then the bite of the North wind reminded him that he had to continue his journey to Troll Castle. "I almost forgot about Spike," he said, as he set off into the wind toward the Glen.

The Nisses had finally returned to the safety of the Nisse Palace. They had finished lunch and Pendulum was packing his oiling can into his Tinkering Belt.

"It certainly is wonderful to visit the Nisse Palace again," Pendulum said. "But now I have to continue to the Royal Palace and find the Magic Compass. The Nisse Palace could be next on the Prince's list."

"Be careful, Pendulum," Balto cautioned. "Fennika could be anywhere."

"I'll be careful, and if everything goes according to plan, I may be back in time for supper."

"And be careful that the humans at the Royal Palace don't see you," Tandara added.

"I'll be doubly careful."

Balto opened the trap door in the floor and Pendulum disappeared into the burrows that would take him to the Royal Palace.

"Good luck," Tandara whispered as Balto closed the trap door.

Clipper decided to climb the tower and check on all the palaces that had disappeared while they were away.

Early that afternoon Miranda and the Prince were out for a ride in the Royal Sleigh. The two horses trotted along the forest paths. The Prince had insisted that Miranda accompany him to the Christmas tree forest.

"You will choose your favourite tree in front of my eyes, so there'll be no mistake," he said smiling. "And I'll have witnesses to make sure. You won't be able to play games anymore."

Miranda's voice was as frosty as the air. "I don't play games, Your Highness."

The sleigh came around a bend. "Stop the sleigh!" she shouted. "Stop!"

The Prince reined in the horses and the sleigh came to a halt.

"What's the matter?"

"Where is it?" she cried.

"Where is what?"

"The White Palace. Where's the White Palace? It should be over there."

"I made it vanish," the Prince said laughing.

Miranda jumped from the sleigh and the Prince followed her. "But Pendulum lived in the White Palace. You destroyed his home," she cried, as she traced with her footsteps the outline in the snow where the White Palace once stood.

"Who's Pendulum?" the Prince asked.

"A Nisse," Miranda answered.

The Prince threw his arms into the air. "Not again. Not more talk about Nisses."

"It's so typical of you," Miranda shouted. "Uncle Klo is right. You never listen to anyone but yourself. He says your father was a good listener and -"

"Yes, I know, and his father before him. Miranda, how many times do I have to tell you that I am who I am. I know I make some mistakes along the way, but..."

"Some mistakes?"

"All right. I make many mistakes along the way. But they are *my* mistakes. A Prince is like everyone else in the Kingdom."

"In what way could you possibly be like anyone else in the Kingdom?" Miranda asked.

"I have the right to fail, and to learn from my mistakes. And so do you."

"Don't change the subject, we were talking about Nisses."

"Miranda, I want you to stop talking about Nisses. I don't find it funny anymore," the Prince said, returning to the sleigh.

"Of course it isn't funny," Miranda said. "You and that Magic Compass. It's all your fault." Miranda yanked the Magic Compass from around the Prince's neck.

"Miranda, give that back to me! Be careful. It's magic," the Prince warned, chasing Miranda around the sleigh.

"I'm going to destroy it," Miranda threatened, holding the Compass above her head.

"No, wait!" the Prince shouted. "If you give me back the Compass, I'll release Klo."

Miranda lowered her arms. "Do you promise?"

"Yes, Miranda. I promise. But you must promise me something in return."

"What?"

"You must promise to continue the work on the new palace. In nine days it will be Christmas."

"I can't," Miranda answered, leaning against the runners of the sleigh.

The Prince sat down beside her. "Why not?"

"Because you're going to destroy the Nisse Palace."

The Prince gently removed the Compass from Miranda's hands. "What's so special about the Nisse Palace?"

Miranda thought for a moment, then said, "Come with me to the Nisse Palace tomorrow. I'll show you. It's the only way to make you understand."

The Prince didn't answer.

"If you come with me," Miranda continued, "I'll do my best to finish the Christmas Palace by Christmas Day."

"What do you want to show me at the Nisse Palace?" He hadn't been to the Nisse Palace in years.

"I want you to meet some friends. Now come on, it's cold, we should get back to the Royal Palace. You have a promise to keep," Miranda said as they both climbed into the sleigh.

The Prince and Miranda were not alone in the forest.

Fennika had climbed out from the burrows to discover that the trail of the Nisses ended at the White Palace. When the White Palace disappeared, the Nisses' footprints had disappeared as well. She had been sitting behind a rock covered with snow when the Prince and Miranda had stopped in their sleigh. She had overheard everything they said.

"A Magic Compass?" she whispered. "I bet it's shiny. I want it." She climbed up onto the back of the sleigh, out of sight, just as it was pulling away. "But best of all," she said to herself, "these humans will take me to the Nisse Palace. Soon the Nisse Handbook will be mine!"

As the sleigh raced toward the Royal Palace carrying an unwelcome passenger, Archibald had finally returned to Troll Castle. He searched everywhere but he couldn't find Fennika. He was happy, though, to be home with his best friend, Spike.

"Come on, Spike, let's go for a walk. I want to tell you all about my adventures. I'm sure Fennika will turn up soon."

They came to the clearing where Archibald had planted his little Christmas tree. It had grown three feet while he was gone.

"Dreams really do come true," he whispered, giving Spike a big hug as they sat under the Christmas tree. And there they stayed all night.

It had been another busy day in the Kingdom. Would Miranda and the Prince lead Fennika to the Nisse Palace? And would Miranda convince the Prince that Nisses really did exist?

Until tomorrow, good night.

THE SEVENTEENTH DAY OF DECEMBER

Pendulum had followed the signs in the burrow that showed the way to the Royal Palace. As the first light of dawn crept over the Kingdom, he popped up from the trap door, trying not to make a sound, and found himself under the Prince's bed.

There were dust balls under the bed and Pendulum had to pinch his nose to keep from sneezing. The Prince didn't stir. Pendulum began to search the room for the Magic Compass, but he couldn't find it.

He took a look at the sleeping Prince. There, hanging on a chain around the Prince's neck, was the Magic Compass. He tiptoed to the edge of the bed and reached over to grab the Compass. But the Prince turned over in his sleep, and Pendulum had to walk around the bed to the other side. Once again he reached out—but the Prince rolled over again.

Pendulum was losing patience, he couldn't keep running from one side of the bed to the other.

"How am I going to get that Compass?" he wondered, leaning against an open trunk at the bottom of the Prince's bed. But he leaned on the trunk with a little too much force and the lid came crashing down. The Prince just kept right on sleeping.

"I don't think I'll have to worry about waking him up," Pendulum said with a chuckle.

He rolled up his sleeves and hopped up onto the bed. He took a pair of wire cutters from his Tinkering Belt and snipped the Magic Compass from the chain around the Prince's neck. The Prince didn't move. Pendulum dropped the Compass into his Tinkering Belt.

"I did it," he whispered. "I have the Magic Compass!" And he danced a little jig in the middle of the floor. The clock on the wall struck the hour.

Tick-tock   Tick-tock
I hear the voice of the clock
Ticking all the hours away
I must hurry or lose the day

Tick-tock   Tick-tock
Globs of oil and lots of grease

Will stop the Compass
And give us peace

Tick-tock   Tick-tock
December is here
To bring us good cheer

Tick-tock

Pendulum slid under the bed. He opened the trap door and hopped in. For good measure, he gave the hinges on the trap door a few drops of oil from his oiling can.

❄

Meanwhile, in the dining room of the Royal Palace, Miranda and Klo were enjoying breakfast. True to his promise to Miranda, the Prince had released Klo from house arrest and he was now free to travel in the Kingdom. Miranda was busy dipping fresh strawberries into chocolate.

"Isn't it wonderful, Uncle Klo? The Nisses have escaped from the Trolls of the Glen, and you're free."

"They're safe for the moment, Miranda," Klo answered thoughtfully. "But the only way I can stop the Prince from destroying all the palaces is to get the Magic Compass back."

"Then I'll just snatch it from him and smash it to pieces," Miranda offered, sipping her juice.

"No, you mustn't. The power of the Compass is with the owner. And the owner is the Prince. If you stole it and gave it to me, the power would remain with the Prince. If I try to tamper with the Compass, I will turn to stone."

"To stone? What do you mean?"

"Anyone other than the owner who tampers with the Magic Compass will turn to stone."

Miranda puzzled over the problem for a moment. "I can convince him to return the Magic Compass to you," she said.

"How do you plan to do that?"

"I've asked the Prince to come with me to the Nisse Palace today. When he sees the Nisse family, he'll understand the danger of the Magic Compass."

"It isn't that easy, Miranda. The Nisses always hide from humans."

"We'll see," Miranda answered, popping another strawberry into her mouth.

❄

In the stables of the Royal Palace, a stack of hay began to shake. Fennika sat up groggily and shook the straw from her fur. "Where am I?" she wondered, looking around.

Slowly the cobwebs cleared in her head and she remembered. She had stowed away on the back of the sleigh to the Royal Palace. The sleigh was put into the stables for the night and Fennika had slept in the hay.

"I have to get into the Royal Palace and keep a close watch on those humans. They'll lead me to the Nisse Palace," she said, heading for the door. She peeked out into the courtyard and seeing that it was empty, she stepped out into the sunlight.

The Prince was the last one in the Royal Palace to wake up. He yawned and threw on his robe. He crossed to the windows and gazed through his telescope as he did each morning. He liked to check on the Kingdom and the progress of his Christmas Palace. "Great," he whispered, adjusting the focus of the glass, "they'll be starting on the roof in a day or two."

He took a quick survey of the courtyard. "What's that?" he cried, adjusting the focus for a better look, as Fennika's furry shape came into view. "What a strange creature. I've never seen anything like that before in the Kingdom."

The Prince followed Fennika in his telescope as she crossed the courtyard below. He called for his servant to fetch Klo. Within minutes, Klo came rushing into the Prince's chambers, with Miranda following.

"What is it, Your Majesty? The messenger said that I was to come at once," Klo said, huffing and puffing from climbing the stairs.

"There's an odd looking creature in the courtyard and I want you to tell me what it is," the Prince said excitedly.

Klo took a look in the telescope but Fennika was nowhere to be seen. "I can't see anything unusual. Maybe you were dreaming, Your Highness."

"No, I was awake."

"What did it look like?" Miranda asked.

The Prince began to describe the creature he had seen.

"Did you say it had fur?" Klo asked, confused.

"Yes, and it had big eyes and a big nose and big ears."

"Uncle Klo, do you know what this means?" Miranda asked.

"Yes—a Troll! It was Fennika. She's on the trail of the Nisses."

The Prince was baffled. "Trolls? What are you talking about?"

"Your Highness, the Compass—it's gone!" Miranda cried, pointing to the empty chain around his neck.

"Then it would appear that Fennika isn't your only visitor today. Pendulum must be one step ahead of her," Klo said.

"Of course," Miranda said. "Pendulum came to get the Magic Compass."

The Prince looked more confused than ever. Miranda and Klo sat him down on his bed and told him everything that had been happening. And with the events of the morning so far, the Prince was beginning to believe them.

"Now you understand why you mustn't destroy the Nisse Palace. If you make the palace disappear, the Nisses will have no home," Miranda explained.

The Prince was silent.

"But where is Fennika now?" Klo asked, staring out the windows.

"Over here, Dearie," came a strange voice from across the room.

Miranda, Klo and the Prince turned toward the voice. Fennika was standing at the door.

"Look this way," she said. And before they could blink an eye, she opened her fist and blew the powder she was holding into the room.

"Sleeping powder," Klo whispered as he fell to the bed.

"It's a spell," Miranda yawned, falling into a chair.

"Call the guards," the Prince thought as he fell to the floor, his command never reaching his lips.

Fennika stepped over the humans. "That was easier than I thought," she said with glee.

She grabbed the chain around the Prince's neck. "It's gone!" she hissed. "Those pesky Nisses must have been here ahead of me."

She took a canister from her powder pouch and shook powder onto the floor. She bent to inspect the footprints that appeared in the powder. "Well, well, it's my old friend Pendulum."

She followed the path to the trap door and squeezed under the bed. She was much rounder than Pendulum and it was a tighter squeeze. "Surely these footprints will lead me to the Nisse Palace!" she said, opening the trap door and hopping in. "I'm close, I'm close," her voice echoed as she shut the trap door, leaving Miranda, Klo and the Prince fast asleep

Once again Fennika was on the trail of the Nisses. Would she reach the Nisse Palace before the humans awoke and warned the Nisses? And what will happen to Pendulum if he tinkers with the Magic Compass?

Until tomorrow, good night.

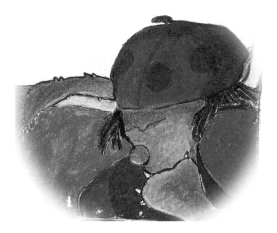

THE EIGHTEENTH DAY OF DECEMBER

The Prince, Miranda and Klo were still under the spell of Fennika's sleeping powder. They had been sleeping for almost twenty-four hours. As the sun rose over the Kingdom once again and the rooster crowed, Miranda and the Prince began to stir.

"What happened?" Miranda asked as she stretched her arms above her head.

"I don't remember," the Prince replied sleepily. "One minute we were talking about Nisses and Trolls and the next thing, I was falling asleep."

"Now I remember," Miranda said. "That Troll, Fennika, ambushed us with her sleeping powder." She ran to her uncle and began to shake him. "Wake up, Uncle Klo, wake up!" she shouted. But Klo didn't budge.

"He must have gotten a double dose," the Prince said.

"We have to find Fennika," Miranda said. "She's probably on her way to the Nisse Palace."

"We can take the Royal Helicopter," the Prince offered.

"Maybe, but we'll have to be careful and watch out for Fennika's tricks."

She turned to her uncle. "I wish Uncle Klo would wake up. He could make up some magic potions in case we run into trouble with the Trolls."

Then she had a thought. "I'll look in Uncle Klo's Book of Charms. Come on."

And before the Prince could answer, Miranda was out the door.

The Nisses were sitting around the table at the Nisse Palace. They were listening to Pendulum's tale of his adventure at the Royal Palace. The Magic Compass was sitting in the middle of the table.

"Can I touch it?" Clipper asked.

"You can play with it after I've finished tinkering with it," Pendulum said.

He reached across the table, picked up the Compass and opened the cover.

"Do you think you can stop the magic?" Clipper asked.

"If it has springs and gears I can fix or unfix it," Pendulum answered. "It's a beautiful Compass." He got up from the table to get a better look in the light, turning the shiny brass instrument over in his hands.

He opened the back cover. "This should be simple, just a few springs to be loosened."

Pendulum began to unwind a spring. Suddenly a great puff of smoke filled the room. When the smoke cleared, Balto, Tandara and Clipper looked at Pendulum. He had turned to stone, still holding the Magic Compass in his hands.

"What happened?" Clipper asked.

"The Magic Compass must have a spell on it. When Pendulum tried to tinker with it, it turned him to stone," Balto said.

Clipper stepped closer to Pendulum for a better look.

"Be careful Clipper," Tandara cautioned, "don't touch Pendulum or you could turn to stone too."

"Is there anything we can do?" Clipper asked.

"Perhaps the Nisse Hand Book has the answer," Balto said, crossing the room to the cupboard.

As Balto and Tandara consulted the Nisse Hand Book, Clipper sat and stared at his uncle. He wondered what it felt like to be made of stone.

Across the Kingdom at the Royal Palace, the Prince and Miranda had entered Klo's laboratory.

"I didn't know Klo had a secret laboratory," the Prince said.

"That's because it was a secret," Miranda replied with a smile.

She was standing beside the Book of Charms. "We'd better find a spell that will protect us against the Trolls' sleeping powder and their other tricks."

She flipped through the pages until she found the one that read: ***How to Protect Yourself from Magic Powders.***

"What does it say?" the Prince asked, peeking over Miranda's shoulder.

"It's very complicated. I hope I can remember everything Uncle Klo taught me," Miranda said, stepping away from the book and closing her eyes.

Blade of fennel   Hair of cat
Ring of onion   Wing of bat
Juice of stone and tail of rat
A little this   A little that

No no no
It won't do
I'm no wizard   Just a fool

But of course—

Juice of stone   Wing of bat

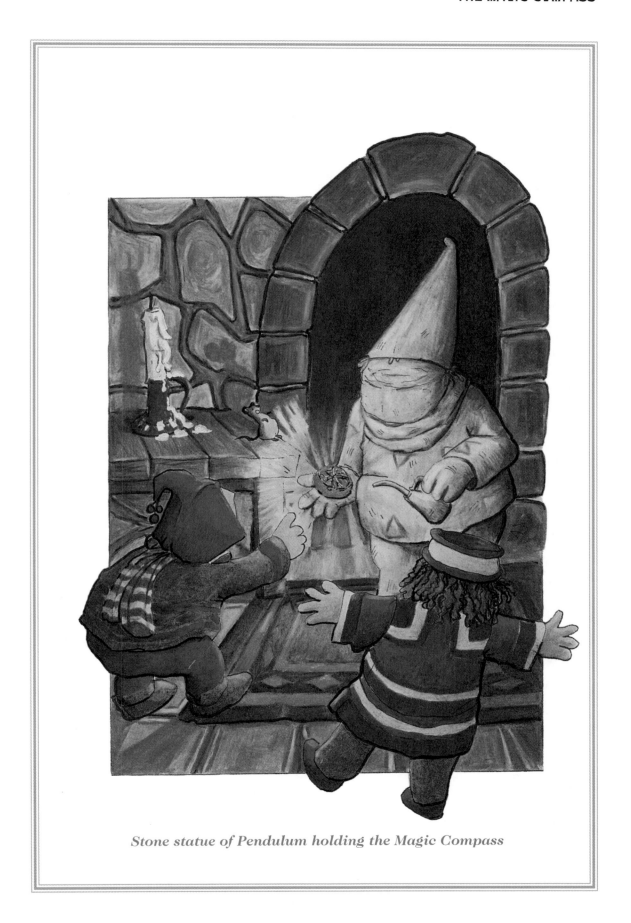

Stone statue of Pendulum holding the Magic Compass

Blade of fennel   Tail of rat
Ring of onion and hair of cat
A little this   A little that

No no no
It won't do
I'm no wizard   Just a fool

But of course—

Mix it once   In this hat
Quill of feather   Ounce of fat
Wipe my feet   On the mat
A little this   A little that

No no no
It won't do
I'm no wizard   Just a fool

But of course—

Wipe my feet Ounce of fat
Mix it once   On the mat
Quill of feather   On this hat
A little this   A little that

Yes yes yes
That will do
I'm a wizard   Not a fool

The Prince looked puzzled. "How do we know it's going to work?"

"We test it," Miranda said. She searched among Klo's jars and found one marked **Itching Powder**.

"Come here," she said, beckoning to the Prince.

"You're not going to test the spell on me, are you?"

"Of course," Miranda answered, sprinkling the Prince with the powder from the jar. "Do you feel itchy?"

"No," the Prince answered, sneezing.

"Then it works," Miranda said. "We're safe from Fennika's magic powders." She replaced the jar on the shelf. "Now we can go to the Nisse Palace."

But the Prince was busy reading the Book of Charms. "Miranda, look. Here's a spell that might send us to the Nisse Palace."

The Prince began to read a passage from the Book of Charms.

This spell can be used to transport a wizard from one area of the Kingdom to another, in the blink of an eye.

"But we're not wizards," Miranda said.

"This is no time to get picky," the Prince replied, as he stepped away from the book. He closed his eyes and began to mumble.

"Maybe we should take the helicopter, after all," Miranda said.

"It's too late," the Prince replied, opening his eyes. "I just recited the spell."

Miranda smiled. "Well, obviously it didn't work. We're still here."

"It says the spell will work in the blink of an eye."

"So?"

"So, I guess all I have to do is blink."

"Wait, don't blink yet. Just in case this spell works, I'd better leave a note for Uncle Klo." She quickly scribbled a note and placed it on top of Klo's Book of Charms.

"Ready?"

"As ready as I'll ever be. But it won't work," Miranda said, closing her eyes just in case.

"Give me your hand," the Prince said. Miranda took the Prince's hand. He smiled, then blinked.

Across the Kingdom, at Troll Castle, Archibald was worried. Fennika still hadn't returned. "Maybe I can find her if I look in the Vat of Boiling Milk," he thought.

He leaned over the vat and stared at the bubbles. "Where is Fennika?"

Slowly the image of his sister appeared in one of the bubbles. "Oh dear," Archibald said, "she's on her way to the Nisse Palace. I have to warn the Nisses."

Archibald thought and thought. Finally he decided to go to the forest and lie down under his Christmas tree until an idea came to him.

Will Archibald find a way to warn the Nisses in time? And will the Prince's spell send him and Miranda to the Nisse Palace?

Until tomorrow, good night.

THE NINETEENTH DAY OF DECEMBER

The next morning, as soon as Archibald awoke, he went back to Fennika's kitchen and peered into the Vat of Boiling Milk as he had done yesterday. Again he saw his sister in a bubble. She was sound asleep in a burrow. Beside her was a sign that said *NISSE PALACE.*

"Spike," Archibald said, "Fennika has reached the Nisse Palace. What are we going to do?"

Spike began to wag his tail and scampered across the kitchen to Fennika's cupboards. He hopped up onto a shelf and began to sniff at the canisters filled with powders.

"What is it Spike?" Archibald asked, crossing the kitchen.

Spike gave another bark and wagged his tail.

"I'm sorry, but I don't understand," Archibald said, shaking his head.

Spike grabbed the canister of powder in his mouth and jumped to the floor, running to the Vat of Boiling Milk. He shook the powder from the canister into the vat.

"Why did you do that, Spike?"

Spike dropped the canister on the floor. Archibald picked it up and read the label on the side. *Sleeping Powder*. Why didn't I think of that? Good dog, Spike, good dog."

He remembered that the powder could travel through the Vat of Boiling Milk and find the creature whose image appeared in the bubbles. And at that moment, it was Fennika who appeared in the bubbles.

"I hope it works," Archibald said.

At that instant, Fennika awoke. It was time to pick up Pendulum's trail after a good night's rest. She was much slower than the Nisses and her trip through the burrows had taken her longer. She sprinkled more of her magic foot powder on the burrow floor.

"Pendulum's footprints end here," she said, looking up and noticing the sign **NISSE PALACE.** "It was right above my head all night!"

She looked to the ceiling of the burrow and spied a trap door. "I found it! I found it!" she shouted, jumping up and down on her short furry legs. "Once I'm inside, I'll steal the Nisse Hand Book. Then I'll steal the Magic Compass and I'll use it to make the Nisse Palace disappear, and all the Nisses with it!"

Nisses are sweet and round and soft
They smile all day and clean the loft
Their homes are filled with light and joy
Good little girls and proper little boys

Nisses are polite and never lie
They never complain they're pleasant as pie
They greet each other with a **how-do-you-do**
They even take baths yes that too

Fennika stopped singing. "It certainly is getting dusty all of a sudden," she said, as she swept the air with her hands. "I think I'll just take a little nap before I go on. Suddenly I feel very tired."

Fennika closed her eyes and slid to the floor of the burrow. Soon her loud snores bounced off the walls. The magic sleeping powder had reached the burrows.

"It worked, Spike, it worked!" Archibald shouted. He had been watching Fennika in the Vat of Boiling Milk.

"The powder should keep her asleep long enough for me to reach the Nisse Palace and warn my new friends. I just hope I don't take any wrong turns in the burrows."

Spike began to yelp.

"Of course you can come with me," Archibald said, "you can follow Fennika's trail with your clever nose."

Spike sprung up and licked Archibald's face. "Wherever I go, you go," Archibald said, shaking Spike's paw.

And off they went to the burrows beneath the castle.

As all this was happening, the Nisses were sitting around the table at the Nisse Palace studying the stone statue of Pendulum. Outside, a blizzard had begun to blow snow against the windows.

Tandara had read the Nisse Hand Book from cover to cover, but she had not found a way to reverse the magic of the Compass and turn Pendulum back into a Nisse.

"Then I'll just have to go to the Royal Palace and ask the Prince to remove his magic spell," Balto said, standing up.

"Are you saying that we make face-to-face contact with the humans?" Tandara asked.

"We have no choice. I'll pay a visit to the Royal Palace and have a word with the Prince."

"The Prince doesn't believe in Nisses."

"Then I'll talk to the wizard. If anybody can help us, he can."

"You'll have to wait until the snow storm stops," Tandara said, looking out the window.

The drifts had already reached the eaves of the palace.

❄

At the Royal Palace, Klo was still sound asleep. Like Fennika, he was under the spell of a sleeping powder.

As for the Prince's spell, it had worked. And in a blink he and Miranda had found themselves in the courtyard of the Nisse Palace. Miranda and the Prince opened their eyes.

"The spell worked, Miranda. We're at the Nisse Palace," the Prince said.

Miranda looked at the palace in front of them. The windows were all lighted with candles. "The Nisse Palace? It looks more beautiful than I remember," she said.

"I must admit, it certainly looks different. It almost looks new," the Prince said, pointing. "Miranda, look over there. That bush. It should be a tall walnut tree. I used to climb in it when I was a child."

Miranda looked at the tiny tree. "But that walnut tree is only a sapling."

"Miranda, all the trees look smaller. Something is very odd here," the Prince said, scratching his head.

Suddenly Miranda gasped. "Your Highness, look at our clothes!"

Miranda wore a long flowing dress, the hem touching the snow.

The Prince looked at his own clothes. He wore a fine cape and breeches, with shiny buckles on his shoes.

"It must have been the power of the spell," the Prince said. "It mixed up our clothes. Let's go inside."

The Prince and Miranda climbed the stairs to the terrace. As they passed the windows they peeked inside and saw an elderly man and woman sitting beside a fireplace. "It's not possible," the Prince said in disbelief, moving away from the window.

"Who are those people?" Miranda asked.

"They're my great-grandparents. I recognize them from the portraits that hang in the Royal Palace. But this is impossible."

"I told you the spell was too powerful. It has transported us to the Nisse Palace all right, but it's the Nisse Palace of a hundred years ago. We've gone back in time."

"What do we do now?" the Prince asked.

"We have to find a way back," Miranda said. "Try repeating the spell. Maybe it will take us back to where we started."

"But I can't remember the words."

"You're just excited, they'll come back to you in a minute," Miranda said, reassuring the Prince. She peeked in the window again. "Are they really your great-grandparents?"

"Yes. My great-grandfather built the Nisse Palace. He was very proud of it. And my grandfather built the Ochre Palace, and my father the Royal Palace. But the Nisse Palace is the most beautiful of them all."

"So that's why you're so eager to build a Christmas Palace," Miranda said. "You want to show the people of the Kingdom that you're as clever as your father and grandfather and his father before him."

"I suppose," the Prince answered, moving away from the window.

"But why destroy everything they built?"

"Because I'm not like them. I'm not clever. Everyone is always comparing me to my father or my grandfather. I thought that if I made all the palaces disappear, everyone would give me a chance without comparing me to them. I don't want to compete with my ancestors."

"But you wouldn't be competing. Your palace shows who you are," Miranda explained. "It's playful and youthful—everyone would be happy there. So there's no reason to destroy the other palaces."

"Klo says I'm irresponsible. He says my Christmas Palace is just a big toy," the Prince said.

Miranda stepped closer to the Prince and took his hand. "I think your Christmas Palace will be beautiful. Maybe when it's finished, it will be the most beautiful palace in the Kingdom."

"You're just saying that. After all, you're building it. It's mostly your ideas."

Miranda gathered her thoughts before she spoke. "At first I was determined to build the palace exactly the way you wanted it. I hoped it would be a failure."

"Why?"

"I was upset because you locked up Uncle Klo. But when I studied your plans, I realized that they were quite good. I could never have designed anything as beautiful. I'm just not a good architect. So it really is your palace."

Miranda stretched up on her tip toes and kissed the Prince quickly on his forehead. "Now, about the spell. Can you remember it?" she asked.

"No," the Prince said, shaking his head. "Not yet."

"Then we better sleep on it. Maybe you'll remember in the morning."

The Prince and Miranda found the stables and bedded down for the night. Miranda slept in the loft above the cows. The Prince shared the manger with the lambs. Within minutes they were sound asleep.

After the Prince had a good night's sleep, would he remember the words to the spell? And how long would the sleeping powder keep Fennika snoring?

Until tomorrow, good night.

THE TWENTIETH DAY OF DECEMBER

Fennika's lingering scent in the burrows had led Spike and Archibald to the Royal Palace.

"This must be where the Prince lives," Archibald said, admiring the palace.

Spike continued sniffing the ground and Archibald followed him around to the side of the palace to an open window. Archibald lifted Spike through the window and climbed in after him. They were in the Royal Kitchen.

"Smell all those cakes and candies, Spike," Archibald said, as he inhaled the fresh aroma of ginger cakes and taffy.

The tables were filled with Christmas baking.

"Where does the trail go from here, Spike?" Archibald asked.

Spike sniffed the air and headed for the hallway. Archibald followed him up the stairs. They came to the Prince's bedroom and Spike found Klo asleep on the Prince's bed. He started to lick the wizard's face.

After three days, the power of Fennika's sleeping powder had worn off and Klo slowly opened his eyes. "What's this? Where did this dog come from?"

"Oh no," Archibald whispered, "it's a human. I better hide."

While Klo was occupied with Spike, Archibald slid under the Prince's bed.

"Down doggy, down," Klo commanded. Spike stopped licking Klo's face and lay at his feet. Klo slowly rose off the bed, his joints were stiff from sleeping for so many days.

"Where am I?" he wondered. "Yes, now I remember, the Troll was here and sprinkled us with her sleeping powder. But where are the Prince and Miranda?"

As Klo searched the room, he spied Archibald's tail sticking out from under the bed. He crept up to the bed and grabbed hold of it. "Ah hah," he shouted, "I've got you!" He pulled Archibald out from under the bed. "Where are my niece and the Prince?" he shouted.

Archibald began to tremble with fright. "Please don't shout at me," he begged. "I'm your friend."

Klo looked at the Troll in surprise. "Friend, what do you mean? First you spray me with sleeping powder and now you say you're my friend? And look at your pockets. You've been stealing Christmas candy from the Royal Kitchen."

Archibald looked at his shirt. A candy cane had stuck there while he was admiring the Christmas cakes and candies. "I'm not who you think I am," Archibald cried. "I'm not Fennika. I'm Archibald."

Klo took a closer look and began to laugh. "Indeed you are," he said, then turned to Spike. "And this is your friend, Spike." He scratched Spike on the belly. "You've been very helpful to the Nisse family."

"Yes, it's true," Archibald answered. "We've been very helpful. But my sister Fennika has been here and she's not so nice. She knocked you out with her sleeping powder. But I don't understand why she came here."

"Fennika hoped the Prince and my niece Miranda would lead her to the Nisse Palace—and to the Nisses," Klo explained.

"Fennika is at the Nisse Palace," Archibald said. "Well, almost."

He told Klo about how he had put Fennika under the spell of her own sleeping powder and that she was fast asleep under the trap door of the Nisse Palace. "I'm on my way to warn the Nisses before Fennika wakes up."

"The Nisse family is safe for the moment, but I don't understand what's happened to the Prince and my niece," Klo said.

"What should we do?" Archibald asked.

"We'll start by having breakfast. I'm sure you're hungry after your long journey, and I haven't eaten for three days," Klo said. "After we've eaten, we'll find Miranda and the Prince."

Beneath the trap door of the Nisse Palace, Fennika began to stir. Archibald had not sprinkled enough of the sleeping powder into the Vat of Boiling Milk to keep her asleep for very long. She wiped the sleep from the corners of her eyes. "I must have been more tired than I thought. Now what was I doing before I fell asleep?"

She saw the trap door above her head and reached up and slowly opened it.

At that moment, the Nisses were gathered around Balto. He had made the decision to go to the Royal Palace. He would ask the wizard to help them reverse the magic of the Compass and turn Pendulum's statue back into a real Nisse.

"Be careful," Tandara said, wrapping a scarf around Balto's neck. "Fennika could be anywhere and it's still storming."

"Yes, yes. Fennika could be anywhere," a raspy voice cried out.

The Nisses turned to see Fennika standing in the middle of the living room.

"Papa, it's Fennika!" Clipper shouted.

"How did she get here?" Tandara asked, "the Nisse Palace is invisible to Trolls."

Fennika began to laugh. "Yes, but the footprints of Pendulum are not invisible. I used my magic foot powder to follow his footprints and they led me to the trap door below the Nisse Palace."

"What should we do?" Clipper whispered.

"I have big Troll ears," Fennika said. "I can hear everything you whisper. Now stay where you are, or I'll spray you with my sleeping powder."

Fennika pointed her canister of sleeping powder at the Nisses. Tandara, Balto, and Clipper backed away from the table and stood huddled by the wall.

"What do we have here?" Fennika asked, spying the stone statue of Pendulum.

"It's a Christmas gift," Tandara said and the other Nisses looked at her in surprise.

"Christmas gift?" Fennika asked suspiciously.

"Yes," Tandara said, "Balto is very good with stone. He made a statue of Pendulum. We're going to give it to him for Christmas."

"And where is Pendulum now?" Fennika asked, raising her eyebrow.

"He...he's collecting holly berries," Clipper said.

"Yes, he's collecting holly berries and we'd better cover the statue before he gets back or it won't be a surprise," Balto said.

"Christmas gift, what a silly idea," Fennika said looking around impatiently. "Where is the Nisse Hand Book?"

The Nisses said nothing.

"If you don't tell me where the Nisse Hand Book is, I'll sprinkle you with enough sleeping powder to keep you dreaming for a hundred years."

"Oh, all right," Balto said, going to the cupboard.

"Balto, you can't give a Troll the Nisse Hand Book!" Tandara cried hurrying after him.

"We have no choice," he sighed, with a wink. He removed the Nisse Hand Book from the cupboard and placed it on the table.

"Finally, the Nisse Hand Book with all its secrets!" Fennika shouted, rushing toward the table.

"And I suppose you want the Magic Compass too?"

"Yes, yes. Give me the Magic Compass!"

"It's over there, in the statue's hands," Balto said, pointing to Pendulum.

Fennika threw back her head and began to laugh. "You silly Nisses, now that I have the Nisse Hand Book, I'll use the Magic Compass to make the Nisse Palace disappear, and you with it. I'll never have to worry about Nisses again!"

She reached out to grab the Magic Compass from Pendulum's hands. But as her furry little paw made contact with the Compass, the spell that had turned Pendulum into a statue, turned Fennika, in another puff of smoke, to stone as well.

The Nisses began to jump and shout.

"We did it!" Balto shouted, "we tricked Fennika!"

"They did it," Archibald shouted, "they tricked Fennika!"

After breakfast, Klo had taken Archibald and Spike to his laboratory. They had watched the adventures of the Nisses and Fennika in the fireplace.

"That was close," Klo said, wiping his brow.

"But what do we do now?" Archibald asked.

"First I must find the Prince and Miranda. Then we'll all go to the Nisse Palace. The Prince will reverse the magic of the Compass. Pendulum will turn back into a Nisse and the palaces will stop vanishing. And not a day too soon. There are only three palaces and one castle left in the Kingdom."

"What about Fennika?" Archibald asked.

"We'll decide what to do with her later."

But as he approached the Book of Charms, Klo wondered where the Prince and Miranda were. Then he read the note Miranda had placed on top of the book. "Oh no," Klo said. "The Prince and Miranda have been tampering with my Book of Charms. They recited a powerful spell that took them to the Nisse Palace. But they chose the wrong spell."

"You mean they didn't reach the Nisse Palace?" Archibald asked.

"Yes and no. The spell they chose sent them back in time."

"Back in time? Is that bad?"

"No, not really. They just have to repeat the spell and they'll return to the present."

But Klo was worried the Prince would not remember the spell.

"I hope they come back soon," Archibald said. "It'll soon be Christmas and we have to stop the magic of the Compass."

"That's right, Archibald. I'll have to find out where in time the spell took them. When I do, I'll go there and bring them back. In the meantime why don't you take Spike to the Royal Kitchen. You can have a glass of milk and some Christmas cookies."

It sounded like a very good idea to Archibald and Spike.

Miranda and the Prince were sitting in the stables of the Nisse Palace. The Prince still could not remember the spell to bring them back to the present.

"Try harder," Miranda said.

"I'm too tired," the Prince answered. "I'll try tomorrow. It's bound to come back to me sooner or later."

"It better be sooner. Tomorrow is the twenty-first of December. It's almost Christmas."

"Yes, it's almost Christmas."

Until tomorrow, good night.

THE TWENTY-FIRST DAY OF DECEMBER

It was noon and Miranda was pacing in the stables, waiting for the Prince to come back with some food. Finally he arrived and shook the snow from his cape.

"Have you remembered the spell yet?" Miranda asked.

"I'm sorry, Miranda, I've tried and tried but it's gone from my mind."

Miranda sat on a trunk in the corner of the stable. "Vanished," she said, "just like the palaces."

"No, we still have some time. The Magic Compass won't make the Nisse Palace disappear until tomorrow."

"That doesn't leave us much time."

The Prince sat beside her. "There's something else bothering you, isn't there Miranda?"

"Yes. There are only three more days until Christmas. Even if we get back in time, I won't be able to finish the Christmas Palace."

"Miranda, forget the Christmas Palace. It's the least of our worries," the Prince said.

He unwrapped the bundle he had brought into the stable. "I crept into the kitchen when no one was looking. I found sausages, cheese and apple cider. Are you hungry?"

"I'm starving," Miranda said and stuffed a big piece of cheese into her mouth.

"And while I was there, I did some eavesdropping. I heard the kitchen staff talking about a Ball my great grandparents are giving at the palace tonight."

"A Ball?"

"Yes, and if we're still here this evening, you and I are going to that Ball."

"But I don't have a gown."

"Maybe there are some clothes in one of these old trunks," the Prince said, opening the lid of one.

"A Ball," Miranda whispered as the Prince began to pull things out of the trunk.

❄

Meanwhile, in his laboratory, Klo was searching the fire for a sign of the Prince and Miranda. He had built a roaring fire.

Archibald sat by Klo and gazed at the flames. Spike slept soundly in front of the hearth.

"I still can't see them," Klo said, as he peered deeper into the flames.

"I hope you find them soon, it's almost Christmas," Archibald said.

❄

The Nisses were staring out a window of the Nisse Palace. Outside, the winds whipped the snow into high drifts.

"It's a real Christmas blizzard," Tandara said.

"Can I go out and play?" Clipper asked.

"You'll have to wait until the storm passes. You might get lost in all that snow."

But Balto couldn't wait any longer for the storm to pass. He had to go now to the Royal Palace and ask the wizard for help. He clutched the handle of the trap door that led to the burrows. A great gust of wind blew up from below carrying snow with it. He slammed the door shut again.

"Oh no," Balto cried, "the burrow is filling with snow. I won't be able to go to the Royal Palace." To himself he said, "I'll have to wait until the storm has passed. By then it may be too late."

He gazed at the calendar on the wall. There were only three days until Christmas.

Clipper gathered some snow from the floor and made snowballs. Tandara was holding several of the garlands they had made, but the arches in the Nisse Palace were already covered.

"I think we made too many garlands," she said, looking around for somewhere to hang them.

Clipper giggled. He took the garlands from Tandara's hand and raced to the statue of Fennika. Carefully he draped them around her neck. Balto and Tandara began to laugh.

"A Christmas Troll," Tandara said, as they danced around the statue of Fennika.

All you need is needle and thread
A bowl of popcorn
And berries I said
Start with the needle
And loop the thread
Oops turn it around
I meant the head

Through the popcorn
Easy you see
Then string the berries
One two three

Continue your chore
And before you know
Look at your feet
They've covered the floor

Garlands Garlands
Berries red and black
Garlands Garlands
Enough to fill ten sacks

As evening descended on the Nisse Palace of a hundred years ago, the Prince and Miranda were busy dressing for the Ball. The trunks in the stable were filled with fine clothes, all of them white.

Miranda had chosen a long flowing white gown that shimmered with silver threads. The collar and cuffs were studded with brilliants. The Prince placed a sprig of holly in her hair and stepped back to admire her.

"You look like a Winter Princess," he said.

"Thank you," Miranda answered, as she pirouetted in the gown.

"Why do you think all the clothes in the trunks are white?"

"It's a tradition that goes back before my father's time," the Prince explained. "This is no ordinary Ball. It's the Silver Ball."

"Silver Ball?"

"Yes, everyone dresses in white and silver to celebrate the frosts of winter," he said, reaching into the trunk. "And don't forget your parasol." He handed Miranda a shimmering white parasol. "It's part of the tradition. All the ladies carry parasols to the Silver Ball."

The Prince extended his arm to Miranda. "It's time to go."

Miranda took his arm and they stepped out into the courtyard. They easily blended in with the guests who had arrived from the four corners of the Kingdom for the Silver Ball.

The women were all in fine white and silver gowns, the white parasols twirling above their heads. The crystal frost that sheathed the courtyard reflected the brilliants on the gowns and sparkled in the silver air like fireflies. Candles burned in all the palace windows and the music from the orchestra filled the clear night air.

The Prince and Miranda entered the ballroom where hundreds of couples were waltzing across the marble floor. "I've never been to such a grand Ball before," Miranda whispered, as the Prince waltzed her expertly around the dance floor.

Klo was still gazing into his fireplace. Suddenly Archibald jumped from his pillow on the floor. "I see something!" he shouted, pointing to the flames.

Klo looked closer, as the faint forms of the dancers began to appear.

The Prince and Miranda at the Silver Ball

"What are they doing?" Archibald asked squinting.

"It looks like a Silver Ball," Klo said, surprised. "Silver Balls were popular when I was young."

"They look like they're dancing," Archibald said. He had never been to a Ball.

"Yes, they are. And look," Klo said, "I see Miranda and the Prince."

Klo hurried to his Book of Charms and flipped through the pages. He hastily mumbled a spell.

"I'll be back in a flash," he said, and before Archibald could say goodbye, Klo blinked his eyes and vanished.

Miranda and the Prince stepped out onto the terrace.

"What a wonderful evening," Miranda said, gazing at the stars above their heads.

"Come, stand here," the Prince said, as he led Miranda under the mistletoe. "I hope you won't run away this time," the Prince whispered as he kissed her.

"No, I won't run away."

At that very moment, Klo appeared on the terrace beside them and tapped the Prince on the shoulder. "Excuse my interruption, Your Highness," Klo said, with a hint of mischief in his eyes.

"Klo, where did you come from?" the Prince blurted.

"Uncle Klo, you found us," Miranda said, hugging her uncle.

"Yes, and not a moment too soon. Take my hands, we have to go back now."

"But the Ball has just begun," the Prince said.

"There'll be other Balls, Your Highness," Klo said. "Hold on."

He blinked, and in a flash they vanished off the terrace, and left the Silver Ball behind.

Until tomorrow, good night.

THE TWENTY-SECOND DAY OF DECEMBER

In a flash, Miranda, Klo and the Prince had left the Silver Ball, and in a flash they appeared in Klo's laboratory. Archibald had welcomed them with mugs of hot chocolate.

The Prince and Miranda had been surprised to see a Troll sitting at Klo's desk. Klo explained that Archibald was an unusual kind of Troll—not like his sister, Fennika.

After a good night's sleep and a change of clothes, they all began to get ready to travel to the Nisse Palace. The snow storm had finally stopped and the sleigh was being prepared for the journey.

If and when they found the Magic Compass, the Prince would turn it over to Klo and the palaces would stop vanishing. It was the twenty-second of December and there were only two palaces and one castle left in the Kingdom: the Royal Palace, the Nisse Palace and, of course, Troll Castle.

The Prince, Miranda, Klo and Archibald all waited anxiously in the courtyard as the horses were harnessed to the sleigh. Miranda was standing at the edge of the courtyard and gazed at the Prince's Christmas Palace, unfinished on the hill. Klo approached his niece and took her hand. "I don't think you'll be able to finish the new palace by Christmas," he said.

"It doesn't seem so important any more," Miranda replied, turning to her uncle. "And I'm sorry that we tampered with your Book of Charms."

"The important thing is that I found you, Miranda, and that both you and the Prince are safe. In a couple of hours everything will be back to normal," Klo said, patting his niece's arm.

But Miranda continued to admire the unfinished palace on the hill.

"Maybe you can finish it by the New Year."

Miranda smiled. "No, I won't finish this palace."

"Oh?" Klo said, searching Miranda's face for a clue.

"I'm not a very good architect," she said. "I know where my real talents lie." She looked at her uncle to make sure he was listening. "I've decided to go back to my studies in magic. I plan to become a wizard after all, Uncle Klo."

Klo hugged his niece. "This is splendid news. I couldn't have asked for a better

Christmas gift."

Miranda and Klo rejoined the others and climbed onto the sleigh. Klo took the reins between his fingers and the horses took off at a trot. Soon they were racing through the forest toward the Nisse Palace.

"Are we going to pass by the Christmas tree farms?" Archibald asked.

"I'm afraid the Christmas tree farms are in the opposite direction," the Prince answered. "Why do you ask?"

"I love Christmas trees. I could spend all my days in the forest."

"When all this business is over, I'll do something about that," the Prince said.

"Uncle Klo," Miranda said, "are you sure you can reverse the spell of the Magic Compass?"

"Yes, the Prince has given the power of the Compass back to me of his own free will. I can easily reverse the magic without turning to stone."

"I can't wait to meet the Nisses," Miranda said happily. "This is certainly turning out to be an exciting Christmas."

"I've never ridden in a sleigh before," Archibald shouted. " I love the sound of the bells on the horses."

The runners are polished
They glisten and shine
The snow is crisp
We'll make good time
The horses are hitched
With harness and bridle
Hurry up Hurry up
We mustn't be idle

The mares are neighing
The birds all sing
The day is clear
The church chimes ring
But best of all
Are the horses' bells
As they jingle and tinkle
Through hill and dell

As the sleigh made its way toward the Nisse Palace, Balto was shovelling snow from the burrow. "It's hopeless," he said, putting the shovel aside. "There's no way I can shovel a path through the burrows. We'll have to wait until it melts."

"But Balto," Tandara said. "It's almost Christmas and there are only two palaces left. Soon the needle will be pointing to the Nisse Palace."

At that moment, Clipper came bounding down the stairs. He had been up in the

tower looking out over the Kingdom through his telescope. "Mama, Papa, there's a sleigh coming this way and Archibald and Spike are on it!"

"Archibald?" Balto exclaimed. "And Spike?"

"Yes, come and look."

Balto and Tandara followed him to the tower. Balto looked through the telescope. "It's the Prince and the wizard and a young woman."

❄

The visitors from the Royal Palace were welcomed by the Nisses and Tandara and Balto invited their guests inside.

"I'm so happy to see you again, Archibald," Clipper said, giving his Troll friend a big hug. "And you too, Spike," he added, scratching Spike's ears.

They all walked around the statues of Fennika and Pendulum. They laughed at the sight of Fennika draped in garlands. Klo looked at the Magic Compass in Pendulum's stone fist. "Not a moment too soon," he said. "The needle of the Compass is pointing at the Nisse Palace."

He waved his hand over the Compass.

> *Juice of stone   Wing of bat*
> *Blade of fennel   Tail of rat*
> *Ring of onion and hair of cat*
> *A little this   A little that*
>
> *Wipe my feet   Ounce of fat*
> *Mix it once   On the mat*
> *Quill of feather   In this hat*
> *A little this   A little that*

Suddenly there was a cloud of smoke and when it cleared, Pendulum and Fennika were themselves again.

The Nisses rushed to hug Pendulum while Fennika tried to unravel herself from the garlands.

"I'm going to sprinkle you all with enough sleeping powder to send you to dream land for a hundred years," she shouted, reaching for her powder pouch.

"Is this what you're looking for?" Klo asked, holding the powder pouch up for her to see.

"Give that to me!" Fennika shouted.

"Catch," Klo said, tossing the belt toward her. But it disappeared in midair.

"My powders," Fennika cried, "my magic powders! Now I'll never get the Nisse Hand Book."

She began to wail and stomp her feet.

"She certainly is upset," Tandara said.

"The Nisse Hand Book is the only thing that Fennika ever wanted," Archibald said, going to his sister and putting his arm around her shoulders.

"Yes," Fennika sobbed, "the Nisse Hand Book."

"Why is the Nisse Hand Book so important to you?" Clipper asked.

"Because it contains the Nisses' biggest secret."

"It contains many secrets," Balto said, "I don't know if there's one that is any more secret than the others."

"Yes, there's one," Fennika said. "It's on the last page of the book."

"The last page?" Tandara said. "The only secret on the last page is…"

But Tandara couldn't finish her sentence. She began to laugh, and Balto, Pendulum and Clipper joined in.

"What's so funny?" Fennika sniffled.

"The last page contains the recipe for Rice Pudding," Tandara said, fetching the book from the cupboard.

"Yes, the Nisses' biggest secret," Fennika sighed. "I've kept my Vat of Boiling Milk boiling for years, waiting for that day when I could make Rice Pudding."

"That's why you wanted to steal the Nisse Hand Book?" Pendulum asked.

"Yes."

"But the recipe for Rice Pudding isn't a secret," Tandara said, "all you had to do was ask. I would have given it to you."

"Trolls don't ask," Fennika said.

"Well, maybe you should try now," Tandara suggested.

Fennika looked at each of the Nisses and mumbled something.

"I didn't hear you," Tandara said.

"I said," Fennika began, louder this time, 'Can I have the recipe for Rice Pudding?'"

"Of course," Tandara answered and quickly copied it from the Nisse Hand Book and handed it to Fennika.

"It's mine!"

"It's everyone's," Tandara replied. "Everyone should have the recipe for Rice Pudding."

The clock struck the hour.

"What about the Magic Compass?" Balto asked, glancing at Klo.

"Everything's under control," Klo said and opened his hand. The Compass had turned to sand. "It will not make any more palaces disappear."

Everyone began to clap. Fennika had finally gotten what she wanted and was no longer a threat to the Nisses. The Magic Compass had been destroyed, saving the Nisse Palace. And before the Trolls returned to the Glen and the others to the Royal Palace, they all had a bowl of Rice Pudding to celebrate.

"I would like to invite everyone, including the Trolls of the Glen, to a special Christmas Eve party at the Royal Palace," the Prince mumbled, between mouthfuls of Rice Pudding. "And I will have an announcement to make."

Until tomorrow, good night.

THE TWENTY-THIRD DAY OF DECEMBER

The Prince, Miranda and Klo had returned to the Royal Palace and the Trolls to Troll Castle. Fennika was busy making Rice Pudding in her Vat of Boiling Milk. She stirred the Pudding with her spoon and sprinkled it with some cinnamon powder from one of the canisters on her shelf. She had thrown away all her magic powders and replaced them with spices.

Archibald and Spike were out in the forest near the castle. Tandara had given Archibald some garlands for his little Christmas tree which now stood tall and full in the middle of the forest. Archibald wrapped the last of the garlands around the tree and stood back to admire it.

In a forest   In a glen
In a field   Or fox's den
There grows a seed
A little each day
Bursting forth on the first of May

Through rains of Spring
And Summer's warmth
Under Autumn's cloak
And wind from North
The little seed
Grows strong and tall
Until that day
It decks the hall

Balls of Glass
Sparkle on green
Presents wrapped with all our dreams
Candy canes dangle
And strings of berries
Adorn your figure
To make us merry

Archibald heard bells and turned to see the sleigh from the Royal Palace. It stopped beside him. Miranda and the Prince stepped down.

"Good morning, Archibald," the Prince said.

"Your Highness," Archibald answered, bowing to greet the Prince. But he bowed a little too deeply and fell into the snow. The Prince helped him to his feet. "This has certainly been a Christmas full of adventure for you, hasn't it Archibald?"

"Yes, Your Highness," Archibald answered, "I've been writing down everything that happened so I will never forget it."

"What a beautiful Christmas tree," Miranda said, walking around Archibald's tree.

"Thank you," Archibald replied, "I planted it myself."

"Really," the Prince remarked, admiring the tree. "Then I've made the right decision."

"Decision, Your Highness?"

"Yes, Archibald, as a reward for your bravery in helping us, I'm appointing you Official Caretaker of the Christmas Tree Farms."

Archibald couldn't believe what he just heard. Before he could find his voice, the Prince continued.

"It's a big job and you'll have to travel all over the Kingdom taking care of all the Christmas trees."

"I can do it," Archibald said, "I'll be very good."

"I'm sure you will, and to get you started, I have a little gift." He handed Archibald a golden hoe tied with a ribbon.

"Thank you, Your Highness," Archibald said, admiring the tool. "Can Spike help me too?"

"Of course he can. He can be your assistant."

"What's that smell?" Miranda said sniffing the air.

"It's Fennika's Rice Pudding," Archibald answered.

"But it smells burnt."

"Well, she's still learning how to cook," Archibald said and they all began to laugh.

The Prince and Miranda climbed back into the sleigh. "Don't forget my party tomorrow. I'll send a sleigh to fetch you," the Prince called back as the sleigh pulled away.

"We'll be there," Archibald said, waving as he watched the sleigh glide over the snow, the bells on the horses filling the clear winter air.

The runners are polished
They glisten and shine
The snow is crisp
We'll make good time
The horses are hitched
With harness and bridle
Hurry up   Hurry up
We mustn't be idle

The mares are neighing
The birds all sing

The day is clear
The church chimes ring
But best of all
Are the horses' bells
As they jingle and tinkle
Through hill and dell

Pendulum was in the tower of the Nisse Palace gazing out over the Kingdom through Clipper's telescope. Balto came into the tower carrying a mug of hot chocolate in one hand. The other hand was tucked behind his back. "I thought I'd find you up here," Balto said, passing Pendulum the mug.

"I've been tinkering around the Nisse Palace all morning," Pendulum said, "I gave Clipper's telescope a spot of oil."

"Do you see anything interesting?" Balto asked.

"It's what I don't see that saddens me," Pendulum replied, with a sigh.

"We're all upset about the White Palace disappearing."

"All my clocks are gone," Pendulum said, "and the mechanical toy I made for Clipper. I wish I had a gift to give him."

"I've got a surprise for you," Balto said. He brought out from behind his back the mechanical toy Pendulum had made for Clipper.

"It's Clipper's toy!"

"Yes, when we were at the White Palace and discovered that the Troll had captured you, I took it to keep it safe."

"Clipper will be so happy, it's one of the best toys I've ever made."

"Clipper is happy just to have you visit," Balto said. "Which brings us to the next item of business."

"Business?"

"Yes," Balto said sitting on a stool beside Pendulum. "Clipper has reached the age where he should start thinking about a trade. Tandara and I think he's ready to become your apprentice."

"But I don't have a workshop any more."

"Of course you do," Balto replied. "The attic of the Nisse Palace will make a perfect workshop for you—and there's lots of room for an apartment up there too," Balto said, giving his brother a big hug. "Welcome to our home!"

On their return to the Royal Palace, the Prince stopped the sleigh at the site of the half-finished Christmas Palace on the hill.

"I'm sorry about the palace, Your Highness," Miranda said.

"There's nothing to be sorry about," the Prince answered. "You can't expect to build a palace in twenty-four days. Besides, you were busy with more important things."

"Still, your plans were very good," Miranda said.

"Thank you, Miranda. But I don't feel good about all the destruction I've caused."

"But we still have our memories of the palaces," Miranda said. "So they haven't really vanished."

"What do you mean?"

"The plans you drew up for the Christmas Palace had touches of all the palaces in the Kingdom. That will help us remember them."

The Prince thought about this for a moment. "Then I'll make sure the palace is built one day."

Miranda smiled. She had a feeling the Prince would keep his word.

But what about the Prince's important announcement? Would it be a happy one?

Until tomorrow, good night.

THE TWENTY-FOURTH DAY OF DECEMBER

It was Christmas Eve. Pendulum, Balto, Tandara, Clipper, Archibald, Fennika and Spike had arrived for the Prince's Christmas Eve party at the Royal Palace.

Pendulum had spent the afternoon in the company of Klo, who had taken him on a tour of his laboratory. Now they were admiring the Prince's fine collection of clocks throughout the Royal Palace. All at once the clocks struck eight and Pendulum and Klo both set their watches.

> *Tick-tock Tick-tock*
> *I hear the voice of the clock*
> *Ticking all the hours away*
> *I must hurry or lose the day*
>
> *Tick-tock Tick-tock*
> *I think all the springs are locked*
> *A dab of oil   A little grease*
> *I must hurry or have no peace*

The clocks continued to ring out all over the palace and were joined by the chiming of the palace bells.

In the kitchen, Fennika had been taking a nap. After ten scorched batches, she had finally mastered the recipe for Rice Pudding. At the Prince's request, she had spent the afternoon preparing heaping pots of Rice Pudding for all the guests.

The ringing of the clocks and the chiming of the bells woke Fennika from her slumber. She gave all the pots a final stir before joining the others.

> *Tick-tock Tick-tock*
> *I hear the voice of the clock*
> *Ticking all the hours away*
> *I must hurry or lose the day*
>
> *Tick-tock Tick-tock*
> *The rice is waiting*
> *The pots are scrubbed*
> *Boil the milk and grab a mug*

Meanwhile, Archibald and Spike were putting the last decorations on the Christmas tree that Miranda had chosen for the party. Miranda climbed the ladder and handed Archibald the star that would hang on the top of the tree.

Balto, Tandara and Clipper came into the room and admired Archibald's fine decorations. They lighted the candles on the tree as the chimes of the bells and clocks announced it was time for the party to begin.

> *Tick-tock Tick-tock*
> *Christmas is here*
> *To bring us good cheer*
> *Tick-tock*

Fennika, Klo and Pendulum joined the others and each took a turn lighting a candle.

Suddenly the Royal Trumpeters entered the room and sounded their horns. They were followed by the Royal Bakers carrying dishes and trays heaped with candies, cakes and cookies.

The Bakers were followed by a parade of valets, each bearing gifts wrapped in shiny papers and bound with ribbons. They placed the gifts under the tree.

The trumpets sounded again and the Prince entered the room, extending his arms to his guests in a warm welcome. "Happy Christmas Eve," the Prince said, greeting his guests.

He looked out over the room. "As you know, there's something important I want to announce this evening," he said. "I have come to a decision."

Klo shook his head and muttered under his breath. "Oh-oh." He was remembering all the trouble the Prince's other decisions had caused, but he joined the others in polite applause.

"I would like to share my good news with all of you," the Prince said.

The sound of the trumpets filled the room. The Prince gestured to Miranda. "Miranda, if you please," he said, beckoning her to join him.

Miranda came to the Prince's side. A silence fell over the room as everyone awaited the Prince's announcement. He took a deep breath and began. "When the holidays are over, construction on the Christmas Palace will continue," he said. "But first I must learn how to build a proper palace, one worthy to replace the palaces my ancestors built before me. I will return with Miranda to the university to become an architect."

Klo was the first to break out in applause. The other guests applauded the Prince's wise decision to further his education.

The Prince turned to Miranda. "And I have my good friend Miranda to thank. Miranda has helped me to realize that it is important for us to follow our hearts. And my heart leads to the university. Thank you, Miranda."

Miranda blushed as everyone applauded. She turned to join the other guests.

"Where are you going?" the Prince asked, with a glint in his eye.

"I thought you were finished, Your Highness."

"I'm not quite finished. There are two other matters to settle," the Prince said.

Decorating the Christmas Tree

"When I said I would continue to build a fine new palace, I didn't mean for myself. I'm happy with the Royal Palace. I've decided to call the new palace Pendulum's Palace. I give it to him as a gift to replace the White Palace which I destroyed."

Tandara, Clipper, and Balto hugged Pendulum. Pendulum bowed to the Prince and the Prince returned the gesture.

"There's one other matter to settle," the Prince said, taking a small box from his pocket. "Happy Christmas, Miranda." He passed the box to her. Inside was an elegant emerald ring. "This ring belonged to my mother," the Prince said.

"Oh, I could never accept it."

"But you must. This ring can only be worn by a Queen," the Prince said. "It's a tradition. My mother and her mother before her, and her mother before her, have all worn this ring."

"But Your Highness, I'm not a Queen."

"And I'm no King. But one day, I will be King and..."

Miranda slowly raised her eyes to the Prince. "And?"

"And one day, you will be my Queen," the Prince said, quickly adding, "with your permission, of course."

The Prince leaned over and kissed Miranda.

"Three cheers for the future King and Queen," Klo shouted.

Fennika blew her nose with a great *Honk!* "Weddings always make me cry," she sniffled, dabbing her eyes.

Then she raised her head and bellowed as only Fennika could do, "Let's eat, the Rice Pudding's getting cold!"

Fennika's Rice Pudding was the best anyone had ever tasted, and the Prince's Christmas Party was the happiest ever.

❄

And as this tale comes now to a merry beginning, everyone in the Island Kingdom wishes you all a very **Happy Christmas**!

Balto

Archibald and Spike

Klo

Tandara

FENNIKA!

The Prince

Clipper

Pendulum

Miranda

RECIPE FOR
CHRISTMAS RICE PUDDING

INGREDIENTS:

6 cups whole milk

1 cup short-grain rice

1/2 teaspoon salt

TOPPING:

butter and cinnamon sugar

(1 1/2 - 2 teaspoons cinnamon to 4 -5 tablespoons sugar, mixed together)

PREPARATION:

Grease pot with butter or margarine. Bring milk to boil in pot, add salt.

Pour in rice while stirring. Lower heat.

Continue to cook for about 50 minutes on low heat, stirring occasionally.

Do not leave unattended or it will burn.

Put rice pudding into bowls. Add a generous dot of butter in centre of each bowl.

Sprinkle with Cinnamon Sugar.

VARIATIONS:

Add skinned, chopped almonds to rice in latter cooking stage.

Or substitute cinnamon topping with stewed apples, apricots,

strawberries or raspberries.

RIS À L'AMANDE

Leftover Rice Pudding also makes a tasty dessert the next day!

Add 1 cup of hot milk, 2 cups of sugar and a dash of vanilla extract

to 4 cups of cold leftover Rice Pudding.

Stir well, making sure mixture is well blended. Add 1/2 cup of

coarsely chopped and skinned almonds. Let cool.

Whip 2 cups of heavy cream until stiff and fold into rice mixture.

Refrigerate for one hour. Serve it with warm (not hot) cherry sauce on top.